BY NICK ELIOPULOS

The Adventurers Guild series (with Zack Loran Clark)
Gulliver's Travels
Minecraft: Zombies!

STEP INTO READING
Escape from the Nether!
Mobs in the Overworld!
Survival Mode!

MINECRAFT STONESWORD SAGA
Crack in the Code!
Mobs Rule!
New Pets on the Block

MINECRAFT WOODSWORD CHRONICLES
Into the Game!
Night of the Bats!
Deep Dive!
Ghast in the Machine!
Dungeon Crawl!
Last Block Standing!

MINECRAFT™
ZOMBIES!

MINECRAFT™ ZOMBIES!

NICK ELIOPULOS

NEW YORK

Copyright © 2022 Mojang AB. All rights reserved. Minecraft, the MINECRAFT logo, and the MOJANG STUDIOS logo are trademarks of the Microsoft group of companies.

Published in the United States by Del Rey, an imprint of Random House, a division of Penguin Random House LLC, New York.

DEL REY and the CIRCLE colophon are registered trademarks of Penguin Random House LLC.

Published in the United Kingdom by Century, an imprint of Random House UK, London.

Hardback ISBN 978-0-593-49851-4
International ISBN 978-0-593-50099-6
Ebook ISBN 978-0-593-49852-1

Endpaper illustration: Kaz Oomori

Printed in the United States of America on acid-free paper

randomhousebooks.com

2 4 6 8 9 7 5 3 1

First Edition

Book design by Elizabeth A. D. Eno

For John, gone but not forgotten

MINECRAFT™
ZOMBIES!

CHAPTER 1

I t was a dark, moonless night when the stranger came to Plaintown.

Bobbie was done with her daily chores, and her baby brother was fast asleep. For the first time all day, the house was still and quiet, and Bobbie found her gaze drifting out her bedroom window.

She saw movement beyond the torchlight.

At first, she thought her eyes were playing tricks on her. It was hard to see anything on a night like this one, when the moon was blocked by dark clouds and the torches set up around town only served to deepen the shadows. She drew closer to the window; she squinted into the darkness.

There—she'd been right. It wasn't a trick of the flickering torchlight, and it wasn't Shepherd Ellis's sheep running loose again. It was a *person* moving out there. But their movements were strange. They shuffled slowly forward, reaching out with both arms as if for balance.

Bobbie thought it might be a zombie. She'd heard stories about them: mindless, rotting creatures with putrid green flesh and sunken black eyes. They were dead things that stalked the night to prey upon the living.

She was revolted—and curious. She leaned in for a closer look.

As she watched the figure, it seemed to totter and sway, like little baby Johnny had when he'd taken his first steps. Then it stumbled, as if tripping over its own feet, and dropped to the ground right beneath a lit torch.

In the light, Bobbie could see the figure clearly for the first time. It wasn't a zombie at all. It was a boy. And he needed help!

Bobbie's parents honked in protest as she ran past them and threw open the front door. She ignored them. She knew very well that it was against the rules for villagers to leave the safety of their homes after the sun went down. But she also knew that she'd be forgiven for breaking the rules if she could help someone in need.

"Hello?" Bobbie said as she approached the fallen figure. "Can you hear me? I'm Barbara—*Bobbie*."

The figure raised his head. "Poison," he said weakly.

The word chilled Bobbie to her core. *Poison.* Did that mean someone had done this on purpose?

"I need to get you to our cleric," she said. "Do you think you can make it? It isn't far." She took his arm and put it around her shoulder, helping him back to his feet. He took shuffling, uncertain footsteps, but as long as she supported his weight, she knew he wouldn't fall again.

She wouldn't *let* him fall.

Plaintown's temple was only a few doors down from her family's home. She didn't bother knocking. Cleric Avery, surprised by the intrusion, rushed down the stone stairs to question her.

"He's been poisoned," Bobbie explained.

The cleric grumbled, gesturing toward a table. Bobbie helped the stranger climb on top of it. His iron armor clanked against the wood surface. In the bright interior light of the temple, she could see how bad he looked. No wonder she'd thought he was a zombie; he looked half dead.

Cleric Avery examined the boy, honking their conclusions at Bobbie.

"Wither?" she said, doing her best to understand the cleric's gestures and utterances. "Is there a cure? Do you have a potion . . . ?"

The cleric's answer surprised her. But she knew better than to ask if they were joking. In Bobbie's experience, Cleric Avery didn't tell jokes.

Bobbie ran out into the night, heading to the northernmost edge of town. That's where the animals were kept: two sheep, twice as many chickens, and a cow named Daisy.

Bobbie had never milked a cow at night before. But this was an emergency, and although Daisy gave her a funny look, the cow didn't complain.

As soon as Bobbie had returned to the temple, Cleric Avery forced the stranger to drink the milk, straight from the bucket.

"Did it work?" Bobbie asked, impatient. "Will he be all right?"

The cleric grumbled in response. The worst of the danger was over—the milk had cured the wither poisoning—but the stranger was still weak. He needed rest.

"In other words, it's time for me to leave," said Bobbie. "I can take a hint, Cleric." But she hesitated on her way out the door, turning back to smile warmly at the villager. "Thank you for your help. I knew I could count on you."

Cleric Avery grumbled again, uncomfortable with her gratitude. The cleric, like most of Plaintown's residents, didn't enjoy surprises, interruptions, or any sort of deviation from their daily routines. And tonight's events were certainly unusual. Adventurers came through the village every so often, usually to trade for goods or to use a crafting station. This was the first time an outsider had really, truly needed the villagers' *help*, though. And Plaintown had delivered.

Bobbie felt a rush of pride and satisfaction. She basked in the glow of a good deed done well.

She might have felt differently, if she'd only known the trouble that the stranger would bring to her life.

CHAPTER 2

Bobbie was good at mending fences.

She'd had a lot of practice. Plaintown was sleepy and simple and small, but it was located right in the heart of open grassland, with no trees or hills or mountains to hide it from view. Bobbie had never seen the village from a great distance, but she could imagine it was visible for miles and miles—especially at night, when its torches would twinkle like stars against a landscape as dark as ink.

Night was when the monsters roamed freely.

She would hear them, sometimes, as she lay in bed trying to fall asleep. The *click-clack* clattering of walking, stalking skeletons. The hiss and scuttle of a spider as it skittered across the roof. Once, she had even seen an Enderman walking through her living room. It had made strange noises, moved some of her parents' furniture around, and then disappeared in a shower of purple starbursts. She hadn't slept a wink that night.

And then there were the adventurers. Unlike villagers, adventurers had no permanent home—and no real responsibilities.

They wandered from place to place, and from what Bobbie had seen, they didn't always prioritize manners along the way. They cut holes into walls and fences to save walking just a few steps. They took whatever they liked from a villager's chest or garden and left their trash behind. They got into fights with monsters—or with each other—oblivious to the damage they caused.

Bobbie couldn't understand that. She would never go around breaking other people's things.

But as long as things got broken in Plaintown, she'd be there to mend them.

"There you go, Shepherd Ellis," she said, and she set a final piece of fence into place. She'd used oak so that her repair job would match the rest of the fence—and everything else in the village. Aside from a bit of stone, all of Plaintown was made of oak. "See? You can't even tell that there was ever any damage."

Shepherd Ellis *hrm*ed and *haw*ed in the garbled language of the village. Bobbie had to pay close attention to get the gist of what the shepherd was saying.

She nodded patiently, squinting in the sunlight. "They can't have gotten far—they never do," she said. "But I'll find your sheep and bring them back. I promise."

As Shepherd Ellis turned to inspect her repair job, Bobbie strolled south, down the dirt road that ran through the town. She waved to several of her neighbors as they milled around the town square, where a large oak tree stood right at the center of the village. They called it the Heart Oak, and villagers often gathered beneath it for gossip before the day's work began. "Good morning, folks!" she said, and they waved back.

The village temple stood across from the tree. Bobbie stepped inside it, calling out, "Cleric Avery? It's me, Bobbie."

The cleric looked up from their brewing stand, where some new potion bubbled and boiled.

"Where's our guest?" asked Bobbie. "Is he feeling better?"

The cleric honked and gestured around in agitation.

"He took off?" Bobbie said. "And left his garbage behind?" Bobbie picked up a stack of discarded dirt blocks from the floor, and she sighed. "So much for gratitude," she said. "I guess he was just another adventurer after all."

Bobbie slipped out the door to continue her rounds. She visited Fletcher Lee, who was running low on feathers, and Mason Bradley, who proudly showed off a stone they had polished to shining.

Cartographer Haven's house appeared empty. "Hello?" Bobbie called. "I'm just checking to make sure you're good on supplies."

There was no answer. Bobbie took a look inside the cartographer's chest—they were almost out of bread; she'd have to bake some today—and then she lingered, looking around the bright room. It was a colorful space, with paintings and potted flowers and a packed bookshelf. She spun the needle on a desktop compass and examined a large map that had been affixed to the wall.

Plaintown was only the smallest dot upon that map. It was almost impossible to fathom that everything Bobbie knew could fit into such a tiny space. The world was so *big*.

And the ocean! Nearly a third of the map was devoted to a swirling expanse of blue. How could there be that much water in all the Overworld?

Bobbie was so engrossed in her thoughts that she almost didn't hear it.

A shuffling sound. The tiniest movement.

Bobbie wasn't alone.

"Hello?" she said, turning around in a circle. She didn't see anyone, so she stopped and listened.

She could barely hear it, but it was there: the faintest sound of breathing.

"Hello?" she said again, alert for any sign of movement. "Is someone there?"

With a gleeful gurgling noise, a small figure launched itself at Bobbie, leaping from atop a nearby bookshelf. Bobbie screeched in surprise as the figure wrapped its arms around her. Caught off balance, she stumbled, landing flat on her bottom. Her attacker laughed as they fell, squeezing her tighter.

She wasn't being attacked, Bobbie realized. She was being *hugged*.

Where her baby brother was involved, it was an easy mistake to make.

"Johnny!" she cried. "You almost gave me a heart attack."

Her brother gurgled happily, as if he'd just won a game that Bobbie hadn't even realized they were playing. She hugged him back, but an instant later he had ducked out of her embrace and run over to the desk, which he proceeded to climb for no discernible reason.

"What are you doing here?" Bobbie asked him. "Do you want to make maps when you grow up? I bet you'd be a great cartographer." She watched to see if he would pick up the compass, but at the moment he seemed more interested in his own two feet.

Bobbie liked to imagine what her brother might grow up to be. She saw potential clues in everything he did. Tap dancing on an anvil? Maybe he'd be a blacksmith. Cuddling up to a tuft of wool? Maybe he'd take over for Shepherd Ellis one day.

As she watched Johnny jump around in front of the great big map of the Overworld, she felt relieved to know one thing for certain: Johnny might be adventurous, but he'd never grow up to be an adventurer. It simply didn't happen; villagers were villagers, adventurers were adventurers, and one couldn't become the other.

A good thing, too. Just the thought of being parted from her brother made her heart hurt.

Cartographer Haven appeared in the doorway, harumphing about the commotion and shooing the siblings back outside. "Sorry!" Bobbie said, laughing as the cartographer shut the door in their faces.

"Bad baby," Bobbie said and wagged a finger, but she was smiling as she said it. "Do our parents know where you are? Do they even know you left the house?"

Johnny giggled before turning and wandering off.

The kid had a habit of wandering. Bobbie tended to find him in the strangest places—climbing on roofs and balconies, chasing chickens, or jumping on beds. Bobbie assumed it was normal behavior for a baby, but it was exhausting to keep up with him. She'd once spent an entire day trying to track him down, only to finally discover him napping inside Leatherworker Shane's cauldron. (Shane still gave them dirty looks, and Bobbie couldn't really blame them.)

She watched him now as he toddled up to the town golem. Goalie was a gentle giant, a construct carved from iron who kept watch over the town. Bobbie slept a little sounder knowing that Goalie was always there, always alert—always ready to protect the village and its inhabitants from any danger that found its way to Plaintown.

Goalie stood a head taller than any villager, and twice as tall as Johnny, with broad shoulders and long, powerful limbs. But Johnny wasn't intimidated by the golem. As Bobbie watched, Goalie held out a flower—a bright red poppy—and Johnny, unafraid, walked up and plucked the flower from the iron giant's grasp.

"Remember your manners, Johnny. What do you say?" prodded Bobbie and, when it was clear that Johnny had nothing to say, she turned to the golem. "Thanks, Goalie."

Without a mouth, Goalie couldn't respond. In fact, it was usually impossible to know what the golem might be thinking. Bobbie thought she saw the golem's eyes glimmer whenever she spoke to it, though.

Johnny ran off toward home—probably plotting all sorts of mischief on the way, but at least he was headed in the right direction. Bobbie continued south, to the outskirts of town and beyond. The dirt road through the village ended in a field of grass and dandelions just past the library. Away from the buildings, Bobbie's view stretched for miles across the flat grassland. There was literally no place for Ellis's sheep to hide; Bobbie saw them grazing beside a small pond.

Conveniently, there were fresh shoots of sugar cane growing along the pond's edge. Bobbie could use them to make sugar for baking . . . and perhaps she could also make a gift of fresh paper for the cartographer, to apologize for her brother's antics. She broke the sugar cane apart with her hands, stashing the material in her inventory before turning her attention to the sheep. "Come on, Bo. Come on, Peep," she said. "Vacation's over. Time to go home!"

Bo gazed mutely at her, while Peep *baa*ed defiantly. Although she might have had that backward; it was hard to tell the sheep apart.

"Oh, fine, we can take a minute," said Bobbie, and she settled down to sit beside the water. "You're both as stubborn as Johnny. And anyway, what's the point of trying to run off? What's out *there* that's so great?" She swept a hand over the plain, which went on nearly as far as the eye could see before finally coming to an end at a distant mountain range.

Bobbie sighed. "I'll tell you what's out there. Chaos and danger. Greedy, reckless adventurers. And things that want to *eat* you." She turned back toward the village. "Plaintown is home, and home is *safe*. You know what's expected of you, today and tomorrow and the day after that. Because nothing ever changes, and—"

Bobbie stopped short. Even as she said the words, she saw that something had, in fact, changed. Something *catastrophic* had happened.

"The tree," she said breathlessly. "The Heart Oak. It's on fire!"

CHAPTER 3

The heart of Plaintown was burning.

As Bobbie ran into the village, she could scarcely believe her eyes. But there was no denying it: The Heart Oak was consumed in a pillar of fire. Hungry tendrils of orange and yellow flicked upward into the sky.

Although . . . not all those tendrils reached skyward. Bobbie could see flames spreading from the tree to the grass that surrounded it. Fire fanned out along the ground.

All of Plaintown was made of oak.

"Our homes are flammable!" Bobbie cried. She turned to the shocked villagers who stood lining the road, watching the scene in mute horror. "We have to do something!"

The villagers bleated in panic. What could any of them do?

Bobbie racked her brain. She mentally kicked herself for not thinking to fill her bucket with water back at the pond—then she kicked herself again for thinking that a single bucket of water could make a difference here.

But what else did she have in her inventory? Some sticks, sugar cane, a few sheafs of wheat . . .

And dirt. She had a whole stack of dirt!

Bobbie sprang into action. She ran in circles around the town square, piling dirt around her as she went. Grass would catch fire, but dirt would not. It would form a barrier between the blaze and the village's many buildings. Bobbie had never been so grateful for dirt in all her life.

When her barrier was complete, Bobbie turned to the nearest villager—it was Cleric Avery. "Have you seen Johnny?" she asked. "Is he safe?"

Cleric Avery honked in confirmation, then tipped a bald head to one side of the road. Johnny, for once, was still. He sat atop Goalie's shoulder, watching the fire alongside a cluster of villagers. Bobbie joined them, squeezing Johnny's foot as she sidled up beside Goalie. Together, Bobbie and her neighbors stood shoulder to shoulder, bearing silent witness as the fire slowly burned itself out.

The danger, at least, was over. But the Heart Oak—which had stood longer than anyone could remember—was gone. *Consumed.*

Bobbie wondered if she should say something. She cast about for words of solace or wisdom, but they wouldn't come. The silence stretched on, heavy with sadness and shock.

And then, to her surprise . . . a stranger broke the silence.

"Dude! That was *epic*," said a boy. "Way more dramatic than I expected." The stranger stepped through a throng of startled villagers, right over Bobbie's makeshift barrier of dirt, and toward the empty patch of charred ground where the tree had been.

It wasn't just any stranger, Bobbie realized—it was *the* stranger.

The one she had helped the night before. She'd thought he'd left, but here he was, obviously fully recovered. He *must* be feeling better, because he was *grinning*. Grinning, at a time like this.

"Excuse me," Bobbie said, stepping forward and raising her voice above the whispered fretting of her neighbors. "But . . . what are you doing?"

The boy appeared momentarily startled. "Whoa. You're real," he said. "Not gonna lie—I kinda thought I hallucinated you."

Bobbie frowned. "Of course I'm real. And . . . and I don't want to seem *rude*, but I asked you a question."

The boy, clearly less concerned with being rude, gave her a long, curious look. "What are you? Some kind of mutant nitwit?"

"*Excuse* me?" said Bobbie.

"No offense," said the boy—but Bobbie was offended all the same. "It's just, you don't look like any kind of villager I've ever met. You sure don't *sound* like one. But you act like you live here or something."

"I do live here," she said. "This is my home. That tree had stood here for generations. You . . . you didn't have something to do with that fire, did you?"

"Well, sure," said the boy. "I started it."

Bobbie gasped, as shocked by his attitude as by the information. "How could you?"

"It wasn't hard." He smirked. "See, you just need flint and steel, and then you—"

"No," said Bobbie. "No, I mean—I mean *why* would you—?"

"Well, funny story," said the boy. "Did you know you can get charcoal from burning wood in a furnace?"

"What?" said Bobbie.

"Charcoal," said the boy. "It's useful for all sorts of things.

You can create it if you burn wood in a furnace. But that's time-consuming." He turned away from her to look around on the ground. "I thought maybe I'd get a lot of charcoal really fast if I skipped the furnace and just set a big tree on fire. But . . . nope. No such luck." He shrugged. "Oops."

"Oops?" Bobbie echoed. She could scarcely believe it. "There's coal right under our feet! If you dig in any direction, you'll find more than you could ever use. And you—you destroyed an ancient tree that we all cherished so you could make *charcoal*? And it didn't even *work*?"

"That's a melodramatic way to put it," the boy said glibly. "But . . . yeah? I guess?"

Bobbie felt a wave of outrage well up in her chest. And she wasn't alone. At her back, the agitated voices of her neighbors rose into a cacophony of aggrieved honks.

"Whoa!" said the boy, chuckling. "That doesn't sound good. What's got them all worked up?"

"I think you'd better leave," said Bobbie. "I'm sorry, but you're not welcome here."

This only made the boy laugh harder. He had a wicked laugh, Bobbie thought. It sounded cruel.

"I'm not ready to leave," he said. "Not yet. I've still got a lot of chests to loot. Some sheep to shear. And I think I saw a golem around here? Those things drop iron ingots, you know."

"Don't you dare hurt Goalie," Bobbie said, her voice as hard and cold as she could make it.

The boy tittered. "You named the golem? Wow, you are such a freak."

"And you've overstayed your welcome," said Bobbie. "*Leave.* I . . . I won't tell you again."

"Tell you what," the boy said. "Why don't you make me?" And at that, he drew a sword.

It was the most intimidating weapon Bobbie had ever seen, shaped out of diamond, with an edge so thin it looked like it would slice the very air. A subtle purple aura encompassed the glittering, sky-blue length of the blade.

Bobbie took an involuntary step back, unsure what to do. And in her momentary hesitation, a streak of movement and color flashed before her eyes. At first, she thought it was the sword.

But it was Goalie. The golem had leaped forward, stepping between them and smashing a massive fist into the boy, who stumbled back and fell to the ground.

Bobbie gasped. "Goalie, no! Don't hurt him."

The boy looked furious. He glared up from the ground, gazing hatefully from Goalie to Bobbie and back again. "Fine," he said. "I know when I'm not wanted." He stood, putting his sword away and dusting himself off, and Bobbie could see where his armor was now dented. "This is a stupid village, anyway."

As the boy stalked off, the gathered villagers parted to let him pass. He reached out in spite and knocked the hat right off Librarian Clarke's head. Goalie tensed and took a step forward, but Bobbie put a steadying hand on the golem's elbow. They didn't need any more trouble.

"You'll be sorry," said the boy as he stepped off the road and onto the plains. "Sorry you treated me like this. Sorry you ever met me!"

Bobbie didn't say it out loud, but as she turned to look at the empty space where the Heart Oak used to be, she thought: *Sorry to meet you? I already am.*

CHAPTER 4

Not far away and deep underground, an aspiring hero named Ben realized he'd been robbed.

He'd slept poorly, dreaming that he was caught within a massive web. Its sticky threads thrummed and jostled, and Ben knew what that meant: Some monstrous spider was skittering somewhere nearby, just out of sight, making its way across the web, its mandibles dripping with venomous saliva as it approached him, hungry for his flesh . . .

He awoke thrashing in his bed, tearing at the tangled sheets. It took him a long moment to realize that it had only been a dream—that he was *safe*.

A moment after that, he realized that he was alone.

He rose, puzzled over the absence of his friend. "Logan?" he called, but quietly, fearful of attracting the wrong kind of attention. He decided he'd better retrieve his weapons before doing anything else.

"That's not good," he said, peering into his bedside chest. It was where he'd stashed all his valuables before bedding down for the night. He'd had ores and ingots and redstone dust; potions and arrows and arrows that had been treated with potions; a diamond pickaxe, and an enchanted sword. And emeralds! A whole stack of beautiful, glittering emeralds.

It was gone now. All of it, gone.

"Ohh, that's *really* not good," he said again. "Logan?" he called. "Buddy?"

He had to try, but he wasn't expecting an answer, really. Logan hadn't just disappeared—his bed was gone, too, packed up and hauled off along with all of Logan's stuff. And, yes, apparently all of Ben's stuff, too.

"Logan!" he said, shrill this time.

Something answered, but it wasn't Logan.

From the darkness, a harsh hissing sound set Ben's nerves on edge. He knew precisely what he'd see when he turned to face the sound—a creeper skulked toward him. Its eerie alien face was a mask of horror, its downturned mouth open in a frozen, silent scream.

Ben took one instinctive step forward, lifting his sword arm—

Which was empty. Right.

He followed through on his swing anyway, striking the creeper with his bare hand. The mob faltered for a moment, knocked backward by the force of the blow, and Ben thought: I can do this.

And then the creeper exploded.

Ben felt the pain of the explosion and then the disorientation of being thrown off his feet. Grainy smoke filled his vision, and the ground beneath him seemed to disappear. He fell a short distance, taking even more damage upon landing.

It took a few moments for Ben's head to clear. When it did, he realized he had fallen into a lower, darker cave. He was surrounded by the stony rubble left behind in the creeper's explosion. One of the torches from above had fallen by his foot, the explosion having knocked it right off the wall where he'd placed it the night before. He snatched it off the ground and set it upright.

In the small halo of light cast by the torch, Ben gathered up the loose blocks of stone. Aside from the armor he'd been wearing as he'd slept, the stone was all he had in the world. And his armor had seen better days. His simple iron breastplate was pitted and pockmarked; it had probably saved his life just now, but it couldn't take many more hits like that one.

He was hurt, but worse than the physical pain was the knowledge that he'd been abandoned. Ben had known something like this could happen—Logan had *warned* him that he needed to start pulling his weight in their partnership. And Ben had tried, hadn't he? He knew he'd tried.

Tried and failed, apparently.

Ben's gloomy musings were interrupted by the sound of growling in the darkness.

Regrets and remorse would have to wait. Between Ben and the relative safety of the sunlight were an unknowable number of monstrous mobs intent on tearing him to bits. He was unarmed, underequipped, and barely armored, and the only sources of light he had available to him were the torches that he and Logan had left behind the day before. Retracing their steps would be his best chance of surviving . . . and, perhaps, of reuniting with his lost friend.

It was a plan, anyway. He still didn't love his odds. But if he got out of this alive, he'd have a pretty great story to tell.

And maybe that would be enough to prove to Logan, once and for all, that Ben had what it took to be a hero like him.

CHAPTER 5

In the days that followed the burning of the Heart Tree, the memory of the stranger's words and actions hung over Plaintown like a curse.

But days became weeks, and as Bobbie returned to her routine, the boy was soon forgotten, more or less.

He'd left his mark, though.

Bobbie now started her days by checking on the town square. She had removed the makeshift dirt barrier, and the grass had grown back quickly after that. The tree itself was another matter, and not so easily fixed. Bobbie had planted four small saplings, in the hope that they would intertwine as they grew. Maybe, one day, they would grow into a great tree to rival the one that had been lost. But that day, if it ever came, was a long way off.

"Come on, little ones," she coaxed. "Grow big and strong. You can do it!"

Farmer Briar honked at her.

"Bone meal? Where would I get bone meal?" she asked. "It's not like I'm going to fight a skeleton."

The farmer honked again, and Shepherd Ellis chimed in to agree.

"Well, I appreciate the vote of confidence, you two," Bobbie said. "I'll keep it in mind."

Night came early. The midday sun had barely begun its slow dip toward the western horizon when it disappeared behind a thick wall of clouds.

Bobbie felt a chill as the daylight went suddenly dim. "There must be a storm coming," she said.

She had no idea.

The wind picked up, and thunder pealed in the distance. Bobbie hurried to finish what she was doing. She'd strayed from the village again, to a small cluster of oak trees. The trees stuck out from the flat plain like a single tuft of unruly hair—or like a hand grasping upward from the grave. Bobbie had come here to replenish her supplies—she could never have too much oak—but as a bolt of lightning flashed on the horizon, she decided to cut her errand short. Getting caught in a thunderstorm could be dangerous, and not just because of the elements. Sometimes, if the cloud cover was thick enough, nocturnal creatures would come out during a daytime storm. Somehow, Bobbie didn't think her wooden axe would do much good against a monster.

The first drops of rain tap-danced across her shoulders as she crossed into the village. She passed Goalie, who stood watching the plains for signs of danger—or maybe the golem was just intrigued by the lightning. As always, Goalie was oblivious to the rain, making no effort to seek shelter. Bobbie was glad the golem couldn't rust.

As she hurried toward the center of town, Bobbie saw her

neighbors running to and fro, all in a rush to finish their tasks. "It's going to be a big one, I think!" she said to the weaponsmith, who stood at an anvil, putting the finishing touches on a new sword. The villager grunted in agreement.

Window shutters clacked in the wind. Farmer Briar's crops swayed wildly. Lightning flashed overhead, and Bobbie ran the last few yards to her home, swiftly closing the door behind her. Through the window, she could see the drizzle become a downpour; she'd made it indoors just in time.

"Whew," she said, leaning against the closed door. Her parents looked up, startled by her sudden entrance. They offered her a bowl of soup.

"Thanks, that sounds good," she said. "But where's Johnny?"

Her parents honked.

"What do you mean you don't know? There's a storm out there!"

They muttered defensively.

"Then put a bell on him!" she said. "He can't be out there unsupervised all the time."

Bobbie huffed. She braced herself. Then she threw open the door and ran out into the rain. Within a second, she was drenched—exactly what she'd hoped to avoid.

Johnny was going to get a good scolding. She just had to find him first . . .

There was no choice but to go door-to-door. She knew he wouldn't be outdoors. She checked with the shepherd and the farmer, the cartographer and the librarian. None of them had seen her brother.

Thunder rumbled angrily over the village, and Bobbie grumbled with it. She was soaked through; her boots felt heavy and squished with every step. And she still had a dozen buildings to check!

It was getting darker out, too. She could scarcely see a thing.

A flash of lightning gave Bobbie a fleeting view of her surroundings. She saw a figure standing in her path, right in the middle of the dirt road. It couldn't be her brother—even Johnny wasn't reckless enough to wander around in a storm like this one. Besides, the figure was too tall to be her brother.

"Cleric Avery. Is that you?" she asked. "Or . . . or Shepherd Ellis?" Her voice sounded faint in her own ears. The figure didn't seem to hear her at all. But it was so hard to see anything . . .

"Hello?" she called, raising her voice to be heard over the storm. "Who's there?"

The figure's head snapped up. She had its attention at last.

She immediately realized her mistake.

"Zombie," said Bobbie, her voice a whisper.

The zombie fixed her with its gaze. Its eyes were dark wells of hunger as it lurched forward. Although it was still some distance away, it lifted its arms as if grasping for her. It uttered a groan, mindless and hollow, like the rumbling of an empty stomach.

Bobbie knew it wanted to eat her.

She spun on her heels and ran. Home wasn't too far. She could make it. So long as she didn't turn around. She just had to trust that the zombie wouldn't catch her—that it wasn't right behind her, closing the distance so that it could grasp her, drag her down, and bite into her . . .

She was so worried about the zombie behind her that she didn't see the one in front of her until it was nearly too late.

It was the groan that saved her, alerting her to the danger in her path. She looked up and saw clutching hands, green with rot, reaching out to receive her. She skidded to a stop, slipping to the ground. The second zombie loomed above her, and she kicked out at it, pushing away and scrabbling back to her feet. She ran in a new direction, now that the path home was blocked.

She ducked into an alleyway. The darkness was unnerving—but it worked to her advantage. Both zombies that had been pursuing her shambled past her hiding place. She held her breath, not daring to exhale until they were out of sight.

Even in her panic, Bobbie realized something important. One zombie was bad luck. Two zombies . . . might be something worse.

A flash of lightning proved her suspicions right—terrifyingly so. In the momentary strobe of light, she saw figures spread throughout town. A dozen, at least. And every one of them was a zombie.

It was a siege. The town was under attack!

Bobbie screamed—and then realized that was the last thing she should have done. She clamped her hands over her mouth, worried that the scream would bring them right to her.

But she was lucky. The peal of thunder masked the sound of her panic. The zombies still shambled mindlessly about the town—she could just see their outlines set against the deeper darkness of the storm.

Her first thought was of Johnny. Everyone else was safely tucked away at home—she had the storm to thank for that—but what about her brother? He would have sought refuge from the storm, too. But as soon as the rain stopped . . . he could step outside and right into a horde of flesh-eating undead mobs.

Bobbie needed to raise the alarm. She had to let everyone know about the danger! She thought about screaming again, but that would only bring the villagers running. They'd be helpless against the horde.

Slowly, carefully, she edged to the end of the alley. Peering into the storm, she could see the town square by the light of its torches. Standing in front of the four saplings was a wooden arch, and hanging from that arch, glinting in the torchlight, was a bell. If Bobbie could ring that bell, the whole town would know there was danger. They'd know to stay indoors—and to keep Johnny indoors, too.

Just one problem: Between Bobbie and the bell, there were at least four zombies. She might be able to get past one or two of them, but four? It was impossible.

And even if she got past them somehow, even if she made it to the bell, the moment she rang it, every zombie in the area would know exactly where to find her. It would be like ringing the *dinner* bell.

She shifted her weight back and forth, considering her options. None of them were good.

"Come on, Bobbie," she whispered. "You can do this. Don't be a chicken."

Chicken. That's what did it. As soon as she said the word, she thought of Farmer Briar's prize-worthy poultry.

If Bobbie was smart and careful—if she did everything just right—those chickens just might save the entire village.

CHAPTER 6

Bobbie knew Plaintown inside and out. She could have drawn a map in her sleep; she could have walked from the town center to the front door of any given building with her eyes closed and without stomping on a single flower.

That's why she decided to destroy the torches.

She had to force herself to do it. Something deep inside her howled at the idea of making the village even darker. But she knew, rationally, that the dark would give her an advantage. It would make her harder to spot as she made her way—carefully, slowly, painstakingly so—to the farmer's enclosure at the north end of the village.

On the other side of the fence, two chickens, Sally and Sue, clucked and cooed, going about their business as if they didn't have a care in the world. "A little warning would have been nice," she whispered at them. "You know, like a cock-a-doodle-do-you-know-zombies-are-invading? That would have gone a long way. Maybe next time?"

Sally clucked lightly.

"Fine," said Bobbie, and she swiped a freshly laid egg. "But I'm taking this!"

Bobbie looked to the north. She couldn't see far—the storm swallowed the normally picturesque view from the farmer's field. But she knew a vast expanse of open grassland stretched before her. Anything might be lurking out there, and normally that knowledge was enough to make her glad for the safety of the village.

But the village wasn't safe now. It would actually be smarter for Bobbie to head out onto the plains than to turn back and try to reach the bell at the center of town.

"Sometimes the smart move is too selfish to even consider," she whispered to herself.

Sue clucked as if agreeing with her.

"You can say that again," Bobbie said, and she clutched the egg to her chest. "Back I go."

Bobbie took care to consider her every step. She stuck close to the buildings, where the shadows pooled most darkly. She was determined to take her time so that she wouldn't make any careless mistakes.

And then the rain slowed, and Bobbie knew she had to hurry. If the storm ended, her neighbors and family might step outside and be overwhelmed.

She picked up the pace, sliding along oaken walls, stepping lightly but swiftly. Within minutes, she rounded a corner, and the town center came into view. Its bell was tantalizingly close, but there were no more buildings to hide behind. Between her and that bell was nothing but open air . . . and the walking dead.

The rain stopped completely, and Bobbie knew she had no more time to waste. She hefted the egg in her hand, testing its weight—and then she let it fly.

With a tremendous splat, the egg shattered against the bell. The bell swung back, then forward, then back again. And as it moved, it sung out:

CLANG! CLANG! CLANG!

Bobbie wanted to cheer. She'd done it! She'd alerted the village to the danger they were in.

But she'd alerted the zombies, too.

Bobbie had hoped the zombies' attention would be drawn to the bell, giving her time to slip away. But one of them had seen the egg as it had soared through the air. And then, with a sweep of its night-black eyes, it had found her.

The zombie groaned loudly, drawing the attention of its companions. Within seconds, every zombie in the square had Bobbie in its sights.

Bobbie spun around. She needed to get indoors. It didn't matter where, and the temple was closest.

But there were zombies between her and the temple.

In that case, the smithy—

But, no. Zombies were closing in from that direction, too.

Bobbie turned around in a tight circle. Everywhere she looked—everywhere she might try to run—there were zombies shambling forward with their arms outstretched, reaching toward her. She stumbled as she spun, tripping over her own feet. The circle of ghouls closed in around her.

She couldn't fight it anymore. She screamed.

Bobbie curled into a ball, desperate to avoid the touch of the undead for as long as she could. She closed her eyes tight. She could hear the zombies' footsteps echoing in the night, almost sounding like the now-distant thunder of the storm.

Only . . . that was strange, wasn't it? The footsteps sounded far too loud—too *heavy*—to belong to a zombie.

She opened her eyes . . . and saw a zombie go flying through the air. There was only one thing Bobbie knew with the power to send a mob flying like that.

Goalie had come to her rescue!

The iron golem was carving a path to her, fighting its way through a cluster of the undead. The zombies all around her shifted their focus to the oncoming threat, turning away from Bobbie and swarming the golem instead.

Goalie's great iron fists swung back and forth, and zombie after zombie was knocked off its feet. Bobbie felt elation at the sight—but it was short-lived. As mighty as Goalie was, the golem was vastly outnumbered. The injured zombies got back up again, rejoining their brethren. They encircled Goalie, punching and clawing and biting at the metallic hide.

Bobbie saw cracks spreading across that hide, as Goalie's shining skin took more and more damage.

That spurred her to action. The closest thing she had to a weapon was her wooden axe; it would have to do. She leaped forward, swinging the tool in front of her, batting zombies aside. They barely noticed her; they kept all their aggressive focus on the golem. But she pressed forward. She had to help Goalie, as Goalie had helped her . . .

Suddenly, her axe shattered against a zombie's skull.

She should have known. The axe had never been intended as a weapon. And she'd worn it down while chopping wood out on the plain.

She searched her inventory for another weapon. There had to be *something*.

That's when Goalie struck her.

Bobbie didn't know what had happened at first. She only knew that she felt pain, and then she was flying backward. She landed right at the door of the temple, almost as if she'd been thrown to safety . . .

She looked back to where Goalie stood. The golem was a head taller than any zombie, but the undead swarmed the construct, climbing atop one another to overwhelm it. Goalie gazed out over the fracas and met Bobbie's eyes. She expected to see the golem's features twisted with rage, or pain, or even fear. But Goalie was as expressionless as ever. Did the golem know it had saved her life? Did that knowledge bring it any peace? Bobbie searched the construct's eyes for answers.

And then a zombie landed the killing blow. Goalie's iron skin cracked and splintered. The golem uttered a final, tortured breath—a sort of stony death rattle—and then shattered.

"Goalie!" she screamed. "No!"

The zombies immediately turned their attention back to her.

Bobbie whirled around, throwing herself against the temple door. It slammed open, and as soon as she'd crossed the threshold, she slammed it shut again. She watched the closed door with mounting dread. Would the zombies pursue her? Or was she finally safe?

Footsteps sounded behind her, and Bobbie lashed out instinctively with her elbows. She caught Cleric Avery right in the face.

"Sorry!" said Bobbie. "You startled me."

The cleric honked with irritation, but upon seeing the state Bobbie was in, their voice softened with concern.

"I'm okay," answered Bobbie. "But . . . they got Goalie."

Cleric Avery's face drooped. They nodded sadly. Then, reaching out to touch Bobbie's shoulder, the cleric promised they were safe here in the temple.

And that was when the door shattered into splinters, and the zombies stormed the building.

CHAPTER 7

The temple's broken doorway spat forth an endless stream of undead. Bobbie and the cleric, both weaponless, were immediately surrounded. Bobbie pushed and punched their attackers, pulling Avery from their greedy, grasping hands. She narrowly avoided the mobs' gnashing teeth.

"We have to move," said Bobbie, and she gripped the cleric's arm and tugged. "Come on!" She ran for the stairs, dragging Cleric Avery along behind her. The villager stumbled but didn't complain.

They took the stairs two at a time, faster than the zombies could follow. Moonlight shone through the yellow stained-glass windows. The staircase was a dead end—eventually, they would run out of stairs—but Bobbie could only deal with one problem at a time.

Suddenly, Cleric Avery began to tremble.

"Don't be afraid," Bobbie said. "It's going to be okay." *Maybe*, she thought.

Avery slipped from her grip, sinking suddenly to their knees.

"Don't stop now. We have to keep moving!" said Bobbie. "They're right behind us, and you—" She squinted to get a better look at the villager in the dim light. "Cleric Avery, are you all right? You look . . . kind of green . . ."

Cleric Avery's head snapped up. Their skin was a mottled, moldy shade of green, and their eyes shone an unnatural red. Roaring with inhuman threat, the cleric lunged for Bobbie.

Bobbie leaped back. Panicking, she did the only thing she could think to do. She punched the stained-glass window beside her, then dove out the window and into the night.

She fell only a short distance before landing on the temple's stone ledge. It was a long way down; she tried not to look below as she crawled along the ledge, intent on putting distance between herself and her undead pursuers.

Cleric Avery, frothing at the mouth, stood in the broken window, groaning with frustration and menace.

Bobbie choked back a sob. She had known the cleric her whole life. She remembered the Potion of Healing the cleric had given her when she'd skinned her knee; she recalled the slightly-less-grumpy-than-usual look on Avery's face whenever a wandering adventurer left them with just the right ingredient for brewing something new.

That person was gone now. Avery must have been bitten by a zombie when they had been surrounded. The change had taken only seconds.

She looked at the sky. The storm had ended, and the clouds had moved on across the plain. Now she could see the moon, low in the eastern sky. That meant it was still early; the zombies had hours to terrorize the village before the sun would drive them away.

For a moment, Bobbie thought about staying on the temple's roof. Out of sight. Out of the way. Out of danger.

Then she heard the sound of wood splintering. It was followed by panicked honking and ravenous groans. The horde had broken into another building. They'd attacked more of her neighbors!

And her baby brother was still out there somewhere.

Bobbie couldn't afford to hide. She had to act.

She hurried across the roof to the far side of the temple. Checking to make sure no zombies awaited her below, she slid to the ground. It hurt, a little, to fall so far. But she could take a little hurt.

She knew now there was no way to survive this night unscathed.

Next door was the smithy, where she'd seen the weaponsmith working on a sword before the siege had begun. She crept onto the open deck, alert for any sign of danger. Peering into a window, Bobbie saw the structure was empty. She hoped the weaponsmith had made it to safety, but she remembered they'd been stubborn about going inside when the rain had started. The zombies might easily have gotten to the weaponsmith before Bobbie had rung the warning bell.

There was a new iron sword sitting atop the anvil. That was some small bit of luck, at least.

Armed at last, Bobbie crouched and snuck to the deck's railing. Chaos reigned over Plaintown. The fletcher's hut had caught fire, casting the whole village in a harsh and eerie light. Zombies were everywhere, shambling up and down the dirt path that ran through town—and now some of those zombies were familiar to Bobbie. The weaponsmith shuffled past, still wearing their apron and eye patch. But their remaining eye glowed red, and their teeth gnashed with unholy hunger as they shuffled aimlessly past their abandoned home.

Home. Bobbie craned her head, but she couldn't quite see her own house from here. She went around to the back of the smithy, walking along the outskirts of town and sticking close to the buildings she passed.

There was no back door to her house, and going around to the front felt too risky. So she hacked her way in—not the best use for a sword, but it was new and sharp and would last for a while.

Inside, her worst fears were confirmed. The house was a mess—furniture was overturned, pictures had fallen from the walls, and all that remained of the front door was broken splinters.

No sign of her parents. But maybe they'd gotten away. Maybe they were okay . . .

Bobbie heard a cry from outside, and she ran to the open doorway. The cry had come from the village cartographer, Haven, who stood trembling on the lawn outside as several zombies closed in.

Bobbie sprang into action, leaping over the porch railing and rushing toward her neighbor. She caught several zombies by surprise, slashing them with her sword and forcing them back. It was enough to give her an opening. She leaned forward, grabbed Haven's arm, and pulled the cartographer free from their attackers.

Bobbie led Haven back toward the house, but the cartographer had other ideas. They pulled against Bobbie's grip, gesturing for her to follow in the other direction.

"Where are you going?" Bobbie asked. "They've taken the whole town."

Haven corrected her in hushed *hrms* and *hahs*.

"Survivors?" Bobbie said. "Gathering at the library?" Her heart swelled with hope. But the library was at the far side of town. "This way," Bobbie hissed, pulling Haven between two buildings, where the light of the moon wouldn't reach them. "We have to be careful! Otherwise we'll lead those things right to the others."

Bobbie took Haven on a twisting, circuitous route through town, staying strictly to the shadows, pausing whenever the sound of shuffling footsteps drew too near. When at last they'd made it to the library, they saw the building's iron door had kept the invading undead at bay. Bobbie had installed that door herself—an attempt at baby-proofing the library against Johnny's mischief. She could see, beside the door, the pressure plate that would open it. But they'd have to fight their way through several zombies to reach it, and after what had happened to Cleric Avery, it felt too risky to drag the cartographer through a gauntlet of ghouls.

"I have another idea," whispered Bobbie, and she drew her sword. "Cover me."

Going around back, Bobbie hacked her way into the library. There was a small group of villagers huddled inside, and, seeing the hole Bobbie had made in their sanctuary, they protested loudly. But one voice rose above all the others—a baby's gurgling cheer.

"Johnny!" cried Bobbie, and she rushed to her brother, sweeping him up in her arms. "Are you okay? Are our parents here?"

Johnny cooed sadly.

"We'll find them," Bobbie promised.

At Bobbie's back, Haven stepped through the hole in the wall, then gestured madly at it, honking for Bobbie's attention.

"Yeah, I know," said Bobbie. She set Johnny down and walked to the hole, plugging it with blocks of oak. "That should hold," she said, and then she scanned the worried faces of the villagers. There were so few of them left. "Is this . . . is this *everybody*?" she asked.

Farmer Briar muttered sadly, and another villager put a pickaxe in Bobbie's hands.

"You want me to do what?" said Bobbie. "Dig us a tunnel out of town?" She shook her head. "We're safer here. I don't *think* those things can break through an iron door. Besides, there might be other survivors out there. We can't just abandon them."

At this, a great cacophony went up, as the villagers argued— with Bobbie, with one another—each one of them determined to voice their opinion on the best course of action.

"That's enough!" said Bobbie, adding her voice to the cacophony. She pleaded for calm, for quiet, but no one was listening.

When fists pounded against the iron door, the villagers at last fell silent. The inhuman growls left no mystery as to who was on the other side of that door. The banging continued.

"They can't break through," Bobbie said again. "I . . . I'm pretty sure." She looked at her brother, then at the tool in her hand. "But maybe we dig, just in case. I could carve out a basement. Put an extra barrier between us and them."

As tireless fists continued knock, knock, knocking on the door, Bobbie set the pickaxe to the ground and dug. She was expecting to find solid layers of dirt or stone beneath the library. Maybe some coal or even iron.

She was *not* expecting light to come pouring up from underground.

"What in the Overworld is that?" she asked, and she bent over for a better look. But before she could make sense of the unexpected sight, a dark, fast-moving shape sprung from the hole. It caught Bobbie right in the face, filling her vision with darkness and causing her to fall backward. The room erupted into chaos, villagers screaming and crying as they scrambled for safety.

"It's a bat," Bobbie said, struggling to be heard over the panic. "It's just a bat!"

But it was too late to calm the crowd. In their panic, desperate to escape, Farmer Briar stepped upon the pressure plate that opened the front door. It was a tragic mistake. Before Briar could take a single step across the threshold, a zombie lunged forward, biting the farmer savagely.

"No!" cried Bobbie, and she crossed the room in three quick strides. Slashing out with the pickaxe, she knocked the zombie back, away from Farmer Briar, just as the iron door slammed shut again, trapping the zombie outside.

And trapping the rest of them *inside* with an infected Farmer Briar.

"Stay back!" said Bobbie, and she held the pickaxe out in front of her. But her hands trembled. She didn't want to use the weapon on her neighbor.

Farmer Briar showed no such hesitation. Mouth frothing, eyes burning red, they lunged for Bobbie. She knew she was done for.

But then Johnny was there. Poor, sweet baby Johnny— foolhardy, fearless, impetuous Johnny—was leaping between Bobbie and her attacker.

Bobbie screamed for him to stay back. But Johnny never did listen to her.

Farmer Briar's attack, meant for Bobbie, found her brother instead.

Bobbie reacted quickly, pulling Johnny out of the zombie's grasp. She carried her brother away from danger, toward the back of the library, where she cradled him in her arms, rocking him back and forth.

"It's going to be okay," she promised. And she thought it might be true . . .

Right until the moment Johnny's eyes turned red.

CHAPTER 8

Bobbie was in a nightmare. None of this was real. That was the only explanation her mind could accept.

But her body knew otherwise. When Johnny lunged for her, she instinctively leaped back.

Johnny kept coming, though. He gnashed his teeth and slashed at the air.

"Johnny, it's me," she said, stumbling backward, staying just out of his reach. "You don't want to hurt me. I'm your sister."

Johnny leaped, and Bobbie did the only thing she could think to do.

She set blocks of wood between them, quickly raising a pillar of oak. Johnny, unable to change his direction mid-leap, slammed into it, falling to the ground. While her brother was dazed, Bobbie quickly dropped more wood, encircling him.

"It's like when we used to build forts, Johnny," Bobbie said, keeping her voice light and calm. "You remember?"

Johnny only growled. She could see the top of his bald head

over the small pen she'd built. It was open at the top—but try as he might, Johnny couldn't hop high enough to get out.

With Johnny no longer attacking her, Bobbie had a moment to catch her breath. She turned to check on her neighbors.

But Farmer Briar's infection had spread unchecked through the crowd. The entire group of survivors had been turned. They stood at the iron door, pounding and scraping, trying to escape out into the night.

Bobbie ducked between two long bookshelves. Grief and hopelessness struck her like a raging river. She felt like she would drown.

But she couldn't give in to despair. Not until she'd seen to her own safety. She blocked off the aisle at both ends, letting the bookshelves on either side of her serve as the walls of her structure—an improvised panic room made of wood and books. She closed herself in completely, using the last of her wood blocks to assemble a low roof just overhead. The space was small and narrow—more like a coffin than a fortress—but with a torch for light it wasn't so scary. She could barely hear the growls of her mindless neighbors through the walls.

Cold comfort, that.

Bobbie slumped to the ground, alive . . . but defeated. She plugged her ears, closed her eyes, and wished for sleep to take her.

But it never did.

And it was a very long night.

CHAPTER 9

Bobbie was in a sort of daze when she realized that sunlight was pouring into the library.

The realization hit her like a bucketful of cold water. She didn't know much about zombies. But everyone knew that zombies and sunlight did not mix.

And her brother was a zombie now. As impossible as that seemed, it was true.

Heedless of any danger that awaited her in the stacks, Bobbie cut her way out of her makeshift shelter. The villagers were all gone—either they'd finally managed to open the iron door, or they'd slipped through the hole in the floor. Bobbie quickly plugged that hole, lest some undead creature reach up from below to grasp at her ankles.

Right now, she only had time to worry about one particular undead creature. Trapped in his wooden pen, Johnny was safe, for now, from direct sunlight. She could just see the top of his green head, turning tirelessly in an endless clockwise circle as he looked for a way out of his one-block-wide prison.

It didn't feel humane to leave him there. So Bobbie blocked the windows, moved a lantern so that its light would better compensate for the lack of sunshine, and then cut away one side of Johnny's enclosure.

He lunged for her immediately.

Bobbie dodged his grasp, quickly shoving him back into his pen and sealing it up once more.

"Okay, that was probably my fault," said Bobbie, her breathing ragged and her knees shaking. "Yeah. Probably should have seen that coming."

Johnny, unseen inside his prison, growled with agitation.

"You're just hungry, aren't you?" said Bobbie. "Well, I understand, I guess, but you can't eat me."

Johnny growled again.

"I'm sorry," said Bobbie, "but that's where I draw the line! Maybe that makes me a bad big sister, but so be it." She sighed. "I'm sure I can find you something to eat that's a little less . . . *me*."

Bobbie walked out into the daylight. All was still and quiet, and for just a moment she could almost believe that the previous night had all been a terrible dream. She turned toward the town center, where her neighbors liked to gather. There was no one there. The broken remains of Goalie lay in the dirt nearby. There was nothing left of her protector but four iron ingots and a poppy flower that looked, from this distance, almost like a bloodstain on the ground. Last night's fires had burned out, leaving several homes in ruins. The remaining structures had all had their doors destroyed. It seemed no one else had escaped the wrath of the zombies.

But maybe she could still save her brother.

The way Bobbie saw it, it was just a matter of education.

She'd already taught Johnny a lot of things in the time since he'd been born. She'd taught him not to pull her hair. She'd taught him to share his toys and not to jump on a bed that was occupied, and she'd even started to teach him the names for different colors.

So teaching him not to eat her shouldn't be *too* hard, she reasoned.

She started with a simple test, setting out a juicy steak in one corner of the library and a fresh-baked cookie in another corner. She opened Johnny's pen and, before he could react, she hurried across the room to occupy a third corner.

Then she waited. Would Johnny go for the dessert? Would he go for the steak?

No such luck. Johnny shambled directly toward her, reaching out as if coming in for a hug—but then, as he got closer, lunging forward with gnashing teeth.

Bobbie was ready for this outcome. She'd covered one hand with an iron boot—it looked funny, and it prevented her from picking anything up, but it at least offered some protection. As Johnny lunged, she held up her arm, intercepting his bite attack with the boot. He gnawed harmlessly on the iron.

"Bad baby," she said. "You won't get any food by attacking me. Wouldn't you like a soft, gooey cookie instead? Look how defenseless it is!"

Johnny growled and grumbled as he slobbered on her boot.

"And don't talk with your mouth full!"

After a few days, the constant growling started to give Bobbie a headache. It reminded her of when Johnny used to cry at all hours of the night. She thought a pacifier of some kind might help.

But what pacified a zombie?

She tried everything she could get her hands on: Honeycomb. A piece of sugar cane. Even an emerald, which might have been a choking hazard, if Johnny still needed to breathe.

He spat everything out of his mouth immediately. Nothing worked.

And then, one day, she found him suckling a bleach-white bone.

"Where did you get that?" she asked, and she reached forward to take it from him. He twisted away from her grasping hands, growling at her and holding the bone close.

"Oh, fine," Bobbie said, watching as her brother gnawed on the bone like it was candy. "It's a little morbid. But at least you're quiet."

Johnny slobbered contentedly.

With the pacifier to calm him, Johnny grew slightly less aggressive in Bobbie's presence, and she considered letting him out of his enclosure a bit more often.

First, she needed to test his instinct for self-preservation. And so, one morning, she opened the library's iron door and threw Johnny's favorite bone outside.

Johnny followed it, stepping right out into the glaring sunlight.

A moment later, he had burst into flame!

Bobbie doused her brother with a ready bucket of water and immediately dragged him back inside. Johnny, slightly charred and completely wet, growled miserably.

"This is for your own good," Bobbie said, and she tied one end of a lead around him. The other end was attached to a wooden post she'd set into the library floor. "It's just until you figure out how to keep yourself safe." Johnny strained at the rope, determined to go back outside and retrieve his bone despite the clear and present danger of the sunlight.

Bobbie sighed. "Something tells me you're going to be on that rope for a very long time."

On his lead, Johnny had a bit more freedom to explore the library. Bobbie watched him, just out of his range. What would he do, now that he could walk around? Would he pick up an old favorite book? Would he play with the enchanting table or try to climb the bookshelves?

Johnny didn't do any of those things. Instead, he knocked the nearest torch off the wall.

"Hey!" said Bobbie. "No!"

Johnny growled. Clearly, he preferred darkness.

"Well, I need to be able to see," Bobbie said, and she set a new torch nearby. "Otherwise you might be able to sneak up on me."

Johnny grumbled. He batted his blood-red eyes sweetly and held out his arms for a hug.

"Aw," said Bobbie, coming closer.

Johnny lunged forward, attempting to bite her. But she was just outside his reach; the lead held, and Johnny's teeth closed harmlessly on the air.

Bobbie sighed, then leaned over and patted him on the head. "We'll keep working on it," she said.

CHAPTER 10

en approached the village with caution.

It was abandoned. That much was certain from a distance. Cobwebs stretched across the empty windows, vines clung to the dark buildings, and an old, neglected fence had fallen apart, allowing whatever animals it once held to roam free. At least one building had been burned down to its crumbling foundations.

But "abandoned" only meant there were no people living there. In the past, Ben and Logan had stumbled upon all sorts of mobs in otherwise empty buildings—zombies, skeletons, creepers, and worse. And without Logan to lead the way, Ben might easily be overwhelmed.

So Ben took it slow. He started in the fields, where crops grew in abundance. He could hardly believe his luck—this bounty could sustain him for a while. If the village's chests were as full of loot as the fields were full of food, he would be able to replenish his inventory in no time.

He cut a melon open with his weapon—a simple sword he'd crafted out of stone—grabbing a slice and devouring it with enthusiasm. It had been too long since he'd eaten fresh food. He wiped the juice off his sword, then put several melon slices in his inventory, keeping one to eat while he walked.

The first house he checked was empty of any threat—which was easy to figure out, because it had no door. Ben stepped inside, crossed to a chest, checked it for traps, and threw it open.

It was empty.

"Slimeballs," he cursed. Empty was *not* what he'd hoped for. But there were a lot more houses to check, and it's not like he had anywhere else to be.

Three houses later, he was beginning to despair. It was clear that someone else had already helped themself to whatever treasure had been here.

At this point, Ben doubted he'd find any loot. But as he looked around the village, he found no shortage of curiosities.

In the town center, four saplings stood unnaturally close together, as if someone had planted them there purposely.

Nearby, a solitary poppy grew. It looked delicate and out of place, a bright pop of red among all the earthy browns and greens.

And, at the far side of town, there was a building with an iron door. Ben tried to peer through the small openings in the door, but the room beyond was dark.

If there was anything of value in this village . . . surely this was where he'd find it.

He lifted his foot above the pressure plate that operated the door.

Then he hesitated.

"Is this a bad idea?" he said. "It's probably a bad idea. Right?"

He looked again at the iron door, wondering what secrets hid behind it.

"Ah, slimeballs. You win again, curiosity," he said, and he put his foot down on the plate.

The door swung open on a dark room. Ben stepped inside and placed a torch beside the door. He saw now that it was a library—or it once had been. The place was in complete disarray, with shelves that had been almost entirely emptied of books, dirt blocks stacked in front of the windows, and a few random blocks of oak strewn about. What had *happened* here?

He heard footsteps in the back of the room.

"Hello?" Ben said. There was definitely someone back there—he could see them moving on the far side of the empty shelves.

"Just a humble traveling adventurer here," Ben said. "No reason to lurk." He took a step forward, then stumbled over a pile of books. "Are you embarrassed about the mess? I'm not really very judgmental. You should see the state of my inventory."

His answer was a low, threatening growl.

Okay, thought Ben. Not a "someone" after all. Some kind of animal?

"Heeere, kitty," he said, creeping forward. "I don't suppose you're guarding a precious treasure back there, are you?"

As soon as Ben reached the edge of the bookshelf—as soon as he had an unobstructed view—he knew he'd made a terrible mistake.

"Zombie!" he cried, and he stumbled backward, narrowly avoiding the grasp of the mob as it lunged for him.

Ben was too surprised to go for his weapon. All he could think of was escape. He scrabbled backward, trying to regain his footing. The zombie's eyes flashed red as it lunged again. Ben flinched, closing his own eyes and bracing for impact . . .

But nothing happened.

Slowly, cautiously, Ben opened his eyes. The zombie filled his vision, grasping for him . . . but it was stuck somehow. It couldn't *reach* him.

Ben got back to his feet, and he realized that he was significantly taller than his attacker. "Aren't you a little *short* for a zombie?" he asked. Ben saw now that it had been left tied to a wooden post. He couldn't quite make sense of that. Unless it had somehow entangled itself by accident?

The zombie growled, swiping impotently at the air.

Ben laughed. "You're like . . . a little baby zombie, aren't you? That's adorable." He drew his sword. "Honestly, I almost feel bad about this."

"Grawr!" said the zombie, and it clacked its teeth in an attempt to bite him.

"See? You get it," said Ben. "Mortal enemies, the two of us, in a fight to the death." He raised his sword, ready to strike the creature down.

"Stop!" shouted a voice, and Ben paused in mid-swing. A girl stood in the open doorway, wearing simple clothes supplemented with an iron helmet and boots. She held a bow, loaded and drawn, but her hands were shaking.

"Don't worry," Ben said, in what he hoped was a reassuring voice. "You're perfectly safe. I'll take care of this monster." He hefted his sword up once more—

And then, suddenly, an arrow was lodged in his chest plate.

Everything went instantly still and silent, as if time itself had stopped. Ben looked down at the arrow, then at the girl, who appeared to be as shocked as he was. Even the zombie had stopped moving to gaze mutely at Ben's injury.

"Ow!" he said at last. "You shot me!"

"I am—*so* sorry," said the girl.

"I can't believe you did that," said Ben. "It hurts!"

"Again, super sorry," said the girl. "But, I mean, I did ask you nicely to stop . . ."

"Not *that* nicely," Ben countered. He plucked the arrow out of his chest plate. It had gone right through the armor but had only nicked his skin. "I thought I was doing you a favor."

"By attacking my brother?"

"That's not your brother. That"—he pointed—"is a zombie."

The zombie attempted to bite Ben's outstretched hand, which Ben felt proved his point.

"He's my brother," said the girl, "*and* he's a zombie." She sighed. "Put your sword away, and I'll tell you all about it."

CHAPTER 11

The girl—Bobbie—did tell him everything.

"I'm sorry," Ben said. "Losing your whole village like that. I—I can't imagine what that feels like." And he truly couldn't. Ben had never stayed in one place for long. He had a hard enough time imagining what it would be like to have neighbors—a *family*—much less what it would be like to have them all swept away in a zombie siege.

"It feels bad," Bobbie told him. "Really bad."

Ben twisted, uncomfortable in the somber silence that followed. He cast about for something to say—something that might lighten the mood.

"Still," he said, and he forced a grin, "you got a pretty sweet house out of the deal."

With an entire village to choose from, Bobbie had decided to stay in the towering temple. Made of stone and built far taller than any of the other buildings, it was more like a fortress than a home. Ben saw the appeal in that. And on a purely aesthetic level, it was an impressive space—grand, even, with high ceilings, stained-glass windows, and colorful banners.

It was messy, though. Bobbie had stacks of books everywhere. This was where the library's missing volumes had gone. And there were potions strewn all over the place, too, including a fresh one bubbling at an active brewing station. It smelled a little off.

Bobbie scowled at him. "If you're trying to get me to look on the bright side, don't." She crossed her arms. "There *is* no bright side. Other than Johnny—who's not exactly himself these days—everyone else I know is gone. They got bitten by zombies and then vanished without a trace."

"They probably burned away when the sun came up," Ben said, and then he saw her scowl deepen. "Uh," he added, "I'm sure it was . . . very quick and painless."

Ben picked up the nearest book and leafed through it. It was full of recipes. When he realized the silence had gone on for too long, he looked up to see Bobbie watching him intently. "What are you doing here, anyway?" she asked him, a note of suspicion in her voice.

"Nothing in particular." Ben shrugged. "The usual."

"The usual," echoed Bobbie. "Attacking harmless kids?"

"*Not* harmless," Ben countered, and he rubbed his sore chest. "Either of you."

"Johnny is literally tied to a post."

"I'm a little biased, I guess!" Ben countered. "Look, I'm a hero. An adventurer! It's sort of my whole deal." He puffed out his chest, flexing a bit, hoping that he looked the part. "That means I fight monsters whenever and wherever I find them. And when I discover a village—abandoned or otherwise—I drop in on it. You know, to resupply."

"To loot the place, you mean," Bobbie said hotly. "I know your kind. You think villagers are just . . . just happy little idiots who exist only to make your lives easier, your adventures more *epic*." She frowned. "Well, our lives matter, and we have some epic times right here at home, you know. This one time, a fox chased a bunny right through the center of town."

Ben waited, assuming there was more to the story. When no more details were forthcoming, he prodded, "And . . . ?"

"*And*," said Bobbie, flustered, "the rabbit got away. I think. I hope."

Ben scoffed. "Too bad for the fox. You know, I once shot a rabbit with an arrow from fifty paces away."

"What?! Why would you do that?"

"To survive," Ben answered in a tone he hoped sounded very grave. "Out there, it's all about survival. And I'd rather be a fox than a rabbit."

"Funny, you strike me as more of a donkey," said Bobbie. "Listen, I don't know what it's like '*out there*,' but I know that *this* was a peaceful place, full of good people who were just going about their business." All the heat went out of her. "We deserved better than to be treated like we didn't matter."

Ben felt suddenly guilty. His eyes fell to the floor. "They mattered," he said. "Of course they mattered. I can tell you for a fact, this village had the best melons I ever tasted."

Bobbie slapped him across the shoulder. "You ate our melons? What is wrong with you!"

"Hey, come on!" he said, ducking her follow-up attack. In doing so, he accidentally knocked the recipe book off the table. "It was a compliment."

"Yeah, well, I'd pass it on to Farmer Briar if I could," said Bobbie. "Just *ask* before you take anything else, okay?"

He picked up the book from the ground, placing it back on the table. "What are you reading? This looks like recipes."

"Potion formulas," Bobbie corrected. "Oh! That reminds me." She hurried over to the brewing stand, removing the bubbling flask and giving it a furtive sniff. "Hm. Hey, would you drink this?"

"I would not," Ben said. He could smell it from a distance, and it did not smell appetizing.

"Yeah, that doesn't look right," Bobbie said, and she placed the flask among a half dozen other failed attempts. "I'm not exactly a natural at this, but I'm *determined* to find a cure."

"Cool," said Ben. "A cure . . . for bellyaches? A cure for sore feet?"

Bobbie rolled her eyes. "A cure for my brother, genius," she said.

"You're looking for a cure for zombieism?"

"That's not a word," Bobbie said. "But . . . yes." She sighed. "That's why I set up in here. Not because it's a 'sweet house.' Our cleric used to live here, and they were really talented at this sort of thing. I guess I was hoping to, I don't know . . . invoke some of their old magic."

"That's not surprising," Ben said. "Clerics are always good with potions." He sniffed the nearest flask, then recoiled. "It's apparently harder than it looks."

"You know other clerics?" asked Bobbie.

"Sure," said Ben. "I mean, not on a first-name basis or anything." He shrugged. "There's a good one just the next town over. Savannaton, I think it was called. Logan and I sold them some rotten flesh a while back. Say," he said, pointing at the flask. "Maybe rotten flesh is the missing ingredient here? It couldn't make it smell any worse . . ."

"There's a cleric? Nearby? And you know where to find them?" Bobbie leaped forward, and Ben shrunk back, expecting to be hit again. Instead, this time, she enveloped him in a hug. "Thank you! Oh, thank you!"

"Oh, sure," said Ben. "I'm sort of getting emotional whiplash, but you're welcome!"

She gripped his shoulders and shook him lightly. She looked a little manic. "Now, how do I get to Savannaton from here?"

"When was the last time you got some sleep? Or a decent meal?" Ben asked her. "I know where you can get a good melon slice."

She shook him more fervently now. "Savannaton," she said. "Where?!"

"Okay, stop!" Ben said, and he pulled out of her grip. "Look, you can't just hop on over to the next town. You have to think about food, and shelter, and it's easier than you'd think to get lost." He shook his head. "And that's not to mention the monsters. You think zombies are bad? There are way worse things out there."

"It sounds like I need a hero," Bobbie said, smirking. "You know. The kind of guy who fights monsters whenever and wherever he finds them."

Ben felt his mouth go dry. He'd definitely oversold his talents. "Well, yeah, but," he said, casting about for an excuse that would allow him to retain some dignity, "it's not like I go *looking* for monsters, and besides, I've got a lot of quests lined up right now, and—"

"I can pay you," Bobbie offered.

"What, in melon?" Ben grinned. "It wasn't *that* good."

"I have emeralds," Bobbie said. "Heroes like emeralds, right?"

Ben did like emeralds.

Ben, in fact, loved emeralds.

He tried very hard not to show it. Logan had taught him that the key to any successful negotiation was to stay cool.

"Eh," he said. "They're all right."

"I also have cake, if you'd prefer," Bobbie offered.

"Tell me more about these emeralds," Ben said, in a manner that was not entirely cool.

"Well, they're shiny—practically new," said Bobbie. "Every time a hero came through, they'd trade emeralds for whatever supplies they needed. But the village didn't have a lot of use for gems—we were mostly self-sufficient—so we kept them stashed away in a safe place." She smirked, as if she could sense Ben's desperation. As if she could smell it. "Escort me to Savannaton and back, and the emeralds are yours."

Ben made a show of weighing the offer, holding out long enough to mask his desperation. "Fine," he said at last. "It's a deal. But when we're out there in the real world, you have to do what I say. No questions asked."

"You got it, hero," Bobbie said brightly. "You're the boss."

Ben, perpetual sidekick, found he liked the sound of that. "That's right," he said. "I *am* the boss." He sighed, noticing the fading daylight through the temple's stained-glass windows. One of those windows was broken, offering an unobstructed view of the late afternoon sky. "I guess we should set out first thing in the morning."

"Johnny can't go out in the sunlight, though," said Bobbie.

Ben narrowed his eyes. "Why does that matter?"

"Because he's coming with us," Bobbie answered. "Obviously."

"Are you kidding?" said Ben. "The kid who tried to eat me earlier today? *That* Johnny?"

"I can't leave him here all alone," Bobbie insisted. "I'm responsible for him."

Ben opened his mouth to argue, but he was struck dumb. How could she possibly think this was a good idea? And why should he go along with it?

Heroes like emeralds, right?

"I'm regretting this already," he said, moaning. "You'll keep him on a leash the whole time, right? A *short* leash?"

Bobbie nodded. Then she saluted. "Whatever you say, boss."

But something in the way she said it this time made him doubt her sincerity.

Suddenly, Ben felt like he wasn't actually the boss of anything.

CHAPTER 12

Ben eyed the zombie boy warily as Bobbie led him out of the library. She had him on a lead, as promised, and at the moment, he seemed docile. Gnawing on a bone, he didn't even acknowledge Ben's presence.

"You see?" she said. "He's very well behaved."

"Right," said Ben. "And you're wearing a boot on your hand because . . . ?"

"It's just a precaution," she said. "Honestly, he barely even tries to bite me anymore."

"Fantastic," said Ben. "Just what I was looking for in an adventuring partner. 'Only occasionally attempts to eat my face.'"

"I think he'd start with your toes," Bobbie said, and at Ben's look of horror, she added, "I'm kidding! It'll be *fine*." As if she could possibly know that. And anyway, if and when they ran into trouble, she clearly wasn't going to be much help—not with one hand gripping a lead and the other stuck inside an iron boot.

"Listen, I took some things from the cartographer's house,"

said Ben, and, holding up a hand to forestall her objection, he added, "Out of necessity, and I'm only *borrowing* them for our errand—I mean, our *quest*."

"'Quest' does sound more impressive," agreed Bobbie.

Ben held up a map. "This is a locator map. I cloned it from another one I left inside the cartographer's house. Long story short, this map will always show the way back to Plaintown, so we don't have to worry about getting lost. It'll even work when we're traveling underground."

"Underground?" echoed Bobbie. "That sounds dangerous."

"Quests *are* dangerous," Ben answered. "If it were up to me, we'd be traveling overland by day, when there are fewer dangers, and camping at night. But we've got your brother's . . . *skin condition* to worry about, so we're going overland by night and underground by day. You have your pickaxe?" Bobbie showed him. "Good, but be sure to remember the first rule of adventuring: *Don't* dig straight down."

"Why not?" asked Bobbie.

"Well, you never know what's directly beneath your feet. And you wouldn't want to drop a tremendous distance, or fall into lava, or land in the grip of an ugly, stinky, slobbering zombie." He turned to Johnny. "No offense." He turned back to Bobbie. "Now, are you sure you grabbed everything of value?" He quickly corrected himself: "Of *use*, I mean. Valuable in a *useful* sense."

Bobbie sighed, stowing her pickaxe and looking through her meager belongings. "It's like I told you before. Every chest in town was ransacked at some point. I think it happened right after the siege, when I was . . . distracted."

"But you definitely have the *emeralds*," Ben said.

"Oh my ghast. Yes!" she said, and she held one out and waved it in his face. "We had them hidden away where no one would look. I promise you're going to get paid."

"I wasn't worried about that," Ben said, fibbing a little. But it's not like he was *greedy*. He could amass a lot of good gear with those emeralds. And good gear meant staying alive—and proving his mettle.

They did not have good gear at the moment. Ben and Bobbie each had a bow, but they only had five arrows between them, which wouldn't last them very long. They also each had one sword and one pickaxe, none of which were of particularly good quality. They would need replacements or upgrades soon. Ben wore his iron chest plate, which had been worn down even *before* Bobbie had added a puncture mark, and he'd cobbled together a new pair of leather boots (so his toes should, in fact, be safe from zombie nibbles). Bobbie had normal, unarmored clothing, aside from her boots and an iron helmet that gleamed in the light of the moon—it had clearly never seen combat. Johnny, of course, wore the tattered remnants of his once-surely-adorable baby clothes.

They would have to be careful. A single hostile mob, if it got the drop on them, could spell their doom.

"Well, nobody lives forever," Ben said glibly. "Should we get going?"

Ben had thought Bobbie would be eager to get started, but she hesitated. "In a minute," she said at last. "Just . . . just give us a minute, first."

Bobbie pulled on Johnny's lead, and the two walked over to the lone poppy growing near the town center. Bobbie kneeled before the flower.

"Thank you for saving me," she said, and she patted her own helmet. "You're still protecting me, even now. I'm taking a piece of you with me." She turned to her brother. "You want to say anything?"

"Grawr," said the zombie boy, who stared blankly ahead with his creepy little eyes.

"He was always good to you," said Bobbie.

Ben tried to give them some space for . . . *whatever* it was they were doing. He turned away from them, twirling his sword in his hand and looking up at the moon. It was a rare moment of peace.

And then Ben was struck from behind. He stumbled forward, barely managing to stay on his feet. That had *hurt*.

"What's the big idea?" he shouted, whirling around.

Bobbie looked up from the poppy. Beneath her helmet, she surreptitiously wiped a tear away. Johnny feigned empty-headed innocence.

"What's the matter?" Bobbie asked.

"Your pet zombie just attacked me!"

Johnny tilted his head, as if confused. "Grr?" he said.

"He did not," Bobbie argued. "I was holding on to his lead the whole time."

"Well, hold it tighter!" Ben said, rubbing his aching back. "We're not going to get very far if he takes a bite out of me every time I turn—look out!"

Ben's warning came too late. A strange creature had dropped from the sky. It had large, tattered wings, eerie green eyes, and exposed bones sticking out along its body. It struck Bobbie from behind, then swooped back into the sky before either of them had a chance to react.

"Ow!" said Bobbie. "Was that a giant bat?"

"Way worse," said Ben, and he held his sword up in front of him. "Phantom." Ben looked up into the sky, where he counted at least five phantoms circling high above them. "When's the last time you slept through the night?"

"I don't know," answered Bobbie. "I mean, my brother's nocturnal, and I've been so focused on looking for a cure. I sort of lost track of the days."

"Well, these things can sense your exhaustion. They strike when you're weak." A phantom swept down to attack him, but he sidestepped, slashing it with his sword as it passed. "Lucky me, now that they're here, they don't seem too picky about who they attack!"

"Ow!" said Bobbie again, dropping Johnny's lead.

Oh, perfect, thought Ben. Now they had to deal with phantoms *and* a zombie that he wasn't allowed to destroy.

But when Johnny leaped into action, it was the phantom he pounced upon—the one that had just struck his sister. He tore into it, and the phantom pounded its wings, taking to the sky in panic.

Had the zombie actually *protected* her? Ben had never seen anything like that happen before.

Then again, maybe Johnny had just lashed out at the nearest moving target. "Could you *please* hold on to that lead?" Ben complained. "We've got to get out of here, and fast." He barely dodged another phantom. "There are too many of them. We've got to dig straight down!"

"But you said never to do that!" Bobbie said.

"Yeah, well, why start listening to me now? Dig, dig!"

Ben struck the dirt beneath his feet, and then the ground was gone and he was falling, hurtling straight down into open space. He opened his mouth to scream—

And then landed on his feet.

"Oh," he said. "That wasn't so bad, actually." Bobbie landed in a heap beside him; Johnny was pulled along on his lead so that he landed right on top of her. Ben helped pull her out from under the zombie while it was still dazed.

"Are we safe from the phantoms?" Bobbie asked as she dusted herself off.

"I don't think they'll follow us underground," Ben answered. "But just to be sure . . ." He leaped up, using dirt to plug the holes they'd fallen through. Now there was no way for the phantoms to reach them. Ben double-checked that Bobbie had a good grip on Johnny's leash, and then he took a breath and surveyed their surroundings.

They'd landed in some sort of tunnel. It had cobblestone floors and walls and a dirt ceiling, and it measured five blocks across by six high—room to maneuver, but far from spacious. Torches were placed along the eastern wall at regular intervals, and a rail ran along the ground.

"Someone built this—and recently, I think," said Ben. He turned to Bobbie. "I've seen mine shafts before, but they're always old and falling apart and full of"—he shuddered—"*spiders*. This is either brand-new or well maintained. Were there any miners in your village?"

She shook her head. "No. Nobody spent any time underground. I would have noticed." She tapped her chin. "It's weird, though. I *did* notice a light coming from underground the night of the zombie siege. After everything that happened, I'd forgotten. But this tunnel must be the source of the light I saw. It must run directly under the library."

"And beyond." Ben peered up and down the tunnel. It continued straight in either direction for as far as the eye could see.

"Well, we may as well take advantage of it. We want to head . . . that way," said Ben, pointing north. But when he turned back to Bobbie, he saw that her gaze was on the ceiling. Some part of her wanted to linger.

"I'm sorry your goodbyes were cut short," said Ben.

"That's all right," said Bobbie, and she forced a smile. "We'll be back soon, right? Just a quick errand-quest first."

"We'll be back before you know it," Ben promised, doing his very best to keep the doubt he felt out of his voice.

CHAPTER 13

t's not forever. That's what Bobbie told herself as she followed Ben down the eerie subterranean path.

She was leaving her village behind. Her home. And because they were underground, she wasn't even sure how far they'd gone yet. Would she still see Cleric Avery's temple rising above the plain if she were up on ground level right now? Or were they past the plains already, and underneath the forest, or even the distant mountains? Bobbie had no idea. But she promised herself she'd be back—just as soon as her brother was cured.

Johnny gurgled and growled from behind her as she dragged him along. It was tiring, keeping him close but not *too* close. She didn't trust Ben to take his lead, though. Johnny was *her* responsibility.

"Okay, hold up," said Ben, and he stopped walking to look at his map. "If we go any farther in this direction, we'll overshoot our mark. We need to veer east. But the phantoms are still a problem if we don't get some rest first. You packed a bed, right?"

Bobbie set her bed down, positioning it against the wall and just beneath a torch. She was glad for the light . . . but also perplexed by it. Somebody had put that torch there, just as somebody had laid the rails. But why?

"I don't get it," said Bobbie. "Aren't you curious about where this rail line goes? Or about who built it? It must serve some purpose."

"I'm not *not* curious," said Ben, and he set his own bed a little farther down the tunnel. "But the Overworld is full of strange stuff. I've seen abandoned mine shafts, deserted temples—structures that somebody must have built for *some* reason. But what that reason could be is anybody's guess." He sat on his bed without removing any of his armor first. "So you can waste brainpower making guesses, or you can focus on survival. I highly recommend the latter, because not surviving sounds like a real drag."

"Better to live in ignorance than to die knowledgeable," said Bobbie. "Got it. Is that lesson number two?"

"That is *not* what I said." Ben huffed. "I only mean that there are things you need to know in order to survive out here. And the purpose of this underground rail isn't one of those things." He pointed at a spot beyond her bed, a good distance from where he sat. "Now set down a fence post, tie your brother to it, and get some sleep. Tomorrow's going to be challenging enough *without* having to worry about phantoms."

Bobbie had thought she'd find it difficult to fall asleep, but the opposite was true. The moment she hopped into bed—before she'd even taken off her helmet!—she fell into a deep, dreamless slumber. Ben woke her by throwing an egg at her, which Bobbie felt was the definition of a rude awakening. "Really?" she said. "You couldn't gently shake my shoulder or something?"

"I couldn't get any closer!" Ben said defensively from a short distance away. He pointed at Johnny, who stood vigilant at the foot of her bed, surrounded by several torches that he had knocked off the wall. "He wouldn't let me get anywhere near you," Ben explained.

"Sweet baby," Bobbie said, patting Johnny's head. "Were you guarding me all night? Don't you need to sleep?"

Johnny growled, and it almost sounded like the purr of a contented cat.

"I scouted around topside," said Ben. "We're near the road that leads into Savannaton."

Bobbie was surprised by that. "You left us down here all alone?" she asked.

"Sure," said Ben. "You looked like you needed the sleep. And 'sweet baby' over there was on guard duty."

Bobbie rubbed her arms, feeling a sudden chill. "I don't think we should split up," she said. "If I'd woken up, and you weren't there . . ."

That seemed to strike a chord of some kind in Ben. His eyes softened, and when he spoke, he sounded unusually solemn. "Hey, I wouldn't abandon you like that. I promise." He rubbed the back of his head. "But you're right. We should stick together. And I found something that might make that easier. Just . . . keep an open mind about it . . ."

Ben seemed suddenly hesitant, and Bobbie found that deeply suspicious. "Go on," she said.

To her surprise, Ben produced a carved pumpkin from his inventory. Hefting it up with both hands, he grinned and said, "What do you think? Is it Johnny's size?"

CHAPTER 14

en felt the carved pumpkin was a marked improvement. "Admit it," he said to Bobbie. "It suits him!"

Bobbie frowned. "He can tell when you're mocking him."

Johnny grumbled, turning from Ben to his sister—and he wobbled slightly. His head was completely enclosed within a pumpkin, which was almost as big as his body, making him a bit unsteady on his feet. The pumpkin's carved smile made the zombie boy appear downright jovial.

"Who's mocking?" said Ben. "It's pragmatic, it's stylish, it's unique. Form *and* function in a single accessory!" He pointed at the sun as it traversed the eastern sky. "Or haven't you noticed that your brother, unique among undead monstrosities, has not caught fire in the light of the sun? That's a pretty good perk."

Bobbie blinked into the sun. "I almost thought you were lying about that."

"Aw, come on," said Ben. "You think I want to see your only brother catch on fire?"

"You want me to answer that truthfully?" she asked, putting her hands on her hips. "Look, I'm glad this means we can travel by daylight." She watched as her brother looked up at the clouds and almost toppled backward. "I just can't help wondering if there's a more . . . *dignified* option here."

"Well," said Ben, "I suppose you could give him your helmet, and *you* could wear the pumpkin." As he talked, he set two blocks of stone down, one atop the other, and then he placed a lit torch on top. At Bobbie's questioning look, he explained, "I like to leave little markers for myself as I travel. If we need to find our way back to the rail tunnel, this should make it a little bit easier to find."

Johnny swatted at the torch, knocking it from its perch.

"I'll try not to take that personally," said Ben.

They traveled a good distance in peace. It was a clear day, with no monsters to be seen (excepting Johnny), and though Bobbie found it necessary to greet every animal they passed, Ben felt they were making good time. At their current pace, they might even make it to Savannaton before nightfall.

But Ben knew better than to count his turtles before they hatched. So he kept his eyes open, scanning the horizon for danger, and he wasn't entirely surprised when he saw a figure on the horizon ahead.

"Hey, heads up," Ben warned. "Someone's coming this way." He drew his sword.

"Is that really necessary?" asked Bobbie.

"Third rule of adventuring," said Ben. "You can't win a sword fight if you're holding a sunflower."

"Sure," said Bobbie. "But a sunflower might help us avoid the fight altogether."

"Better safe than sorry." Ben sighed. "And anyway, what happened to me being the boss?"

"Well, I thought about it some more," said Bobbie.

"I'll bet you did," Ben groused.

"*And*," Bobbie continued emphatically, "I realized that I'm paying you. That means, technically, that *you* work for *me*. Ergo, if either of us is the boss . . ."

"It's you," Ben said, finishing her thought. He stopped walking, forcing her to stop, too. "But you're paying me to keep you *safe*. I can't do that if you don't let me. And—if you don't mind me being honest with you—"

"This ought to be good," said Bobbie.

"—you are *alarmingly* naïve." Ben held up a hand to forestall her argument. "I don't mean it as an insult. It's sort of charming! But that person on the road ahead of us could be an axe-wielding illager, or an adventurer looking to steal our stuff, or a trigger-happy—"

"Trader Riley!" said Bobbie.

"Sure," said Ben. "A trigger-happy Trader Riley would be another example, I guess . . ."

"No, you goof," said Bobbie. "I recognize them." She started running up the path, calling back over her shoulder, "They're a merchant! They come through Plaintown sometimes."

Johnny, pulled behind in her wake, growled and attempted to bite Ben as he passed.

"Yeah, good luck biting anything through that helmet, Chomp Chump," Ben muttered, low so that Bobbie wouldn't hear it.

Ben sheathed his sword and followed behind them, but he didn't hurry. At this distance, he could see that Bobbie was right: The stranger appeared harmless. They wore a fine garment of blue, accented with a glittering gold trim, with a matching hat and simple sandals. Like Bobbie, the trader held a lead, but instead of a zombified sibling, the trader was pulling along two llamas. The llamas wore colorful carpets and aggrieved expressions. But then, llamas always looked a little irate to Ben.

Having been on the receiving end of llama spit more than once, he was not particularly fond of the animals.

As he caught up, Bobbie was giving a tearful, abbreviated account of Plaintown's fate. "They're all gone," she said, and the trader honked and harrumphed in response.

"Wearing the pumpkin? That's Johnny. You remember him. He's just . . . a little under the weather . . ."

Ben could see Bobbie straining to keep Johnny still.

The trader made more noises, and Bobbie chuckled. "His name's Ben. He says he's a hero, but he's sort of more like a mercenary."

"Hang on," said Ben. "Do you . . . you understand each other?" He pointed at the trader. "They're just making gibberish noises."

Bobbie tutted. "First of all, rude. Second of all, just because you don't know a language doesn't make it gibberish." She lifted her chin. "It actually sounds quite poetic to me. And it isn't so hard to get the gist, if you pay attention."

Trader Riley honked in what might have been agreement — or perhaps a very short poem.

"I'll take your word for it," said Ben.

Bobbie turned back to Riley. "He said it's very nice to make your acquaintance. Yes, he's *very* polite for a mercenary . . ."

While Bobbie and Riley continued their conversation, Ben watched Riley's llamas. They appeared especially aggravated, stamping and bleating. They eyed Johnny warily.

Johnny, for his part, had grown unusually still. It was hard to know where his gaze was pointed while he wore the pumpkin, but Ben had a feeling he knew just what had Johnny's attention.

"Uh, Bobbie?" said Ben.

"Just a minute, Ben," she said, her focus remaining on the trader. "That's lovely. How much are you selling it for?"

Bobbie rooted around in her inventory, letting her guard down. It was just for one second—but a second was all it took. Johnny pulled free from her grasp, lunging at the nearest llama, who bleated in alarm.

It was absolute chaos. Johnny, still partially restrained by the helmet, couldn't *eat* the animals, but he swiped at them, tearing into them with his claws. Bobbie shouted for him to stop, the llamas retaliated with copious amounts of spit, and Trader Riley—reasonably enough, in Ben's opinion—chugged a Potion of Invisibility and vanished from view.

"Stop laughing and help me!" said Bobbie. Ben hadn't even realized he'd *been* laughing, but she was right. By the time he reached her side, she had the lead in her hand again and was straining to pull Johnny off llama number one. Llama number two had taken off running for the hills.

"Sorry," Ben said, still chuckling a bit. "But you know, I would have been able to react faster if I'd had my sword drawn and ready, like I'd wanted."

"And who were you going to stab in this scenario?" Bobbie asked sharply, finally pulling her brother away. The llama spat at Johnny one more time before turning tail and running.

"A sword doesn't solve everything," Bobbie continued. "It doesn't solve *most* things."

"It could have solved that llama's attitude problem," Ben countered. "They're all like that, you know. My friend Logan used to run up and slap them. Then he'd hide, so they'd spit on *me*."

"He sounds like a terrible friend," said Bobbie, exhaling as Johnny gave up on pursuing the animals. The lead went slack as he finally settled down.

"What? No," said Ben. "It was a joke—a game." He chuckled again, but this time, it was a little forced. "We were both in on it."

"If you say so," said Bobbie, but her attention was elsewhere. "Johnny, what am I going to do with you? Here, look at this." She produced a seashell from her inventory—a nautilus shell—and waved it at her brother. Johnny remained uninterested, but it caught Ben's eye.

"Where'd you get that?" he asked.

"I just bought it from Riley," said Bobbie. "It only cost five emeralds."

Ben gasped. "You spent five emeralds on . . . *that?*" he said.

"Sure." Bobbie frowned. "Why not? It's pretty. I've never seen—"

"It's useless," Ben said. "We need armor. We need real weapons—my sword is a dull hunk of stone." He pulled his sword out and waved it around to prove his point. "That trader obviously had a Potion of Invisibility. You should have bought that!"

"They weren't offering any potions for sale," Bobbie said. "It was either this nautilus shell or a bucket of fish. Which you'd have known if you'd bothered to interact with Riley *at all* instead of giving those llamas the stink-eye for the last five minutes."

"Ugh, fine!" said Ben, throwing up his hands. "Just . . . just maybe don't spend any more emeralds without talking to me first. At least I know what they're worth."

"You can do whatever you want with the emeralds," said Bobbie, "once you've earned them by completing your part of the bargain." She cast a hopeless look at Johnny. "We can't keep going on like this. I *have* to cure my brother."

"I know," said Ben, chastened. His temper evaporated at the sound of desperation in her voice. "Come on. Savannaton is that way, and the path looks clear." He put his sword away, hoping that would put Bobbie more at ease.

If he had noticed the column of smoke snaking above the horizon, he might have kept it at the ready.

CHAPTER 15

"What *happened* here?" asked Ben, and Bobbie knew the answer. She knew, and she wished she didn't.

"It was a zombie siege," she said.

Bobbie took in the scene. It was a village much like hers, except the building materials were different—the wood a more vibrant red, and terracotta where Plaintown had used stone. But the detail that stood out immediately to Bobbie was the lack of doors.

The homes hadn't been built that way. Something had smashed through them.

Ben looked skeptical. "Are you sure?" he asked. "I mean . . . *another* zombie siege? What are the odds?"

"Could it be the same group of zombies?" Bobbie asked. "Roaming across the land, hitting one village after another?"

"No way," said Ben. He looked up at the moon. "They couldn't make it here in a single night. And they burn up in the sun, remember?"

"Johnny found a way around that problem," said Bobbie, and

she inclined her head toward her brother, who was tied to his post. She'd removed his helmet when the sun had gone down—she couldn't shake the feeling that he found it uncomfortable, even if Ben insisted Johnny had shown no obvious signs of discomfort.

"Well, technically, *I* found a way around it," Ben pointed out. "I don't think a pack of roving zombies is going to figure out the same trick. They're nowhere near smart enough." He turned to Johnny. "No offense, champ."

Johnny growled, straining at his lead.

Ben leaned over and *boop*ed his nose.

Bobbie turned in a slow circle, taking in the damage. There might have been survivors—she fervently hoped there had been—but if so, they seemed to have fled.

She turned to Ben. "Do you . . . think they left anything useful lying around here?"

"Oh ho!" said Ben, in his most obnoxious tone of voice. "Isn't that interesting? Suddenly it's *okay* to take other people's things."

Bobbie scowled. "It's not like that."

"Yeah, well, the moral line is looking a little hazy, is all I'm saying." He smiled. "Come on, I'm teasing. Let's go shopping!"

Ben led the way to the nearest house, practically skipping. He seemed excessively pleased that Bobbie was going along with his looting. Bobbie, for her part, decided she couldn't afford to care. If the villagers had left behind something that could keep them alive—or otherwise help her brother—then she was willing to bend her own moral code.

Ben hopped through an open doorway. As Bobbie watched, she saw a sudden, violent change come over him. Even from behind, without a view of his face, it was unmistakable. His elation was gone in an instant, and a trembling thrum of terror leaped through him nearly as soon as he'd stepped through the open doorway.

"Oh, no!" he cried. "Mercy! Mercy! Oh, help!"

Bobbie ran forward, practically leaping through the doorframe—but then she came to a sudden halt. It wasn't fear or hesitation that held her rooted to the floor. It was a tangled mess of sticky webbing; she was in it up to her waist, and it clung to her fiercely. She could still move, but just barely, and at tremendous effort.

"Where did this come from?" she asked.

"Sp-sp-sp," Ben sputtered. "Spider!"

Ben pointed, directing Bobbie's eyes to a darkened corner of the room. He was right. A large spider crouched in the corner, its black body almost impossible to see in the shadows. But its glittering eyes shone in the dark as it considered what it had caught in its web.

"It's okay," said Bobbie. "I don't think it's hostile."

Ignoring her entirely, Ben drew a bow and fired an arrow at the spider.

"Well, *now* it's hostile," said Bobbie.

Ben shot off two more arrows, but his aim was erratic, and the spider closed the distance quickly, scurrying unimpeded over the webs. As it neared striking distance, Bobbie thought Ben would draw his sword. Instead, he curled up into a ball.

"What are you doing?" Bobbie demanded. And when Ben only whimpered, she added, "What should *I* do?"

"Help!" was all Ben said.

"Oh, this is ridiculous," said Bobbie, and she drew her sword, swiftly cutting the webs away from her body. Clearing a small area, she stepped forward and stabbed out with her sword, slaying the spider with two hits.

"You can come out now," Bobbie said, cutting the webbing away from Ben's crouching form.

"It's gone?" Ben asked, keeping his eyes clenched tight.

"It's gone," Bobbie confirmed. "And it was *way* less dangerous than those phantoms you tried to fight. What just happened?"

"I don't like bugs," Ben said plainly. Bobbie thought he might elaborate, but he only dusted himself off and stepped out into the night. Bobbie scooped up a severed spider eye before following him. She knew they were useful in potions.

After a thorough inventory of the abandoned village, Ben and Bobbie found precious little of use. They managed to collect a few loaves of bread, some rotten flesh, and a gently used shield. (Ben thrilled at the sight.) The cleric, of course, was gone, and they hadn't left behind a single potion.

Ben lingered in the cartographer's home. It was similar to the one in Plaintown, but the large map upon its wall covered a different area. Bobbie noticed that Ben seemed especially preoccupied with a muddy brown region that, she assumed, had to be some sort of swamp.

"What is it?" she asked him.

"It's nothing," he said. Then he shook his head, as if to clear it. "Come on. Let's get your brother and choose a house to stay in for the night. I'll replace the door."

They stepped outside, and Bobbie was overwhelmed by a sense of hopelessness. It didn't matter which house they chose. They were all the same—all husks, emptied of everything that had given them purpose. That was as true for Savannaton . . . as it was for Plaintown.

"You may as well just leave us here," said Bobbie, and she sat right down in the dirt.

"Huh?" said Ben. "Leave you here, in Savannaton?" He made a show of looking around. "Cute place, but there's not much of a nightlife."

"I know this wasn't the deal," said Bobbie. "The deal was that you'd bring us here and take us back again. But what's the difference? Why even go back? There isn't anything for us there." She rooted around in her inventory, pulling out a stack of emeralds. "Here," she said, putting them on the ground between them. "I think that should cover it."

Ben stepped toward the emeralds, but he stopped short.

"Hold on," said Ben. "Was that what we'd agreed to? Are you sure?"

Bobbie looked up at him. "Isn't that enough?" she asked. "It's all I have."

"It's enough," said Ben. He scratched his head comically. "But I thought our deal was that I'd take you back home *after* we'd figured out a cure. We haven't done that yet. Wait—let me check." He ran over to Johnny, extending a hand toward her brother. Johnny attempted to bite him, but Ben was ready for that and too quick, pulling away and leaving Johnny's teeth to *clack* closed on empty air.

Ben ran back to her. "He's still a zombie!" he reported. "So we're not finished yet."

Bobbie searched Ben's face, half expecting this to be a prank of some kind. "Are you—are you serious?" she asked. "I'm pretty sure . . . I thought—"

"Listen, don't go getting all weepy on me," said Ben. "This is just business. Suppose it got around that I took your emeralds and didn't deliver on my end." He clucked his tongue, shook his head. "That sort of negative review can follow a guy around for ages."

Bobbie resisted the urge to leap up from the dirt and hug him. He clearly wanted to maintain the illusion that this was no big deal. But Bobbie knew what he was doing for her, and she was grateful. "I appreciate your professionalism," she said, rubbing at her eyes. "But unless you know where to find another cleric, I'm not sure where we go from here."

"Don't know where to find a cleric," said Ben. "But I might be able to get us the next best thing. I noticed a detail on the map back there." He shook his head. "And this might be a terrible idea, but it's the only one I've got."

"What?" asked Bobbie. "What's the idea?"

"Well," said Ben. "Have you ever met a witch before?"

CHAPTER 16

Bobbie, Johnny, and Ben were off to find a witch. Ben seemed entirely uncertain about this plan—and it had been *his* plan to begin with. If Johnny had an opinion one way or the other, he was keeping his thoughts to himself.

For her part, Bobbie was just happy to have something to do. As soon as they'd started moving again, the despair she'd felt back in Savannaton had fallen away, and new hope had bloomed in the hollow space where all her worries lived. That hope had carried her all through a long day of walking, and on into the night.

Bobbie had always thought that some people were naturally hopeful—that optimism was simply a personality trait. It wasn't until confronted with tragedy that she'd realized the truth: Hope was something you worked for. It took constant effort to seek solutions—to *believe* those solutions were out there—in the face of ceaseless, harrowing problems.

Because you could see the problems. The problems were undeniable. But the solutions . . . those had to be crafted.

They were on a grassy expanse, but it wasn't quite like the plains that surrounded Plaintown. Even in the moonlight, Bobbie could see the grass here was slightly discolored; a less vibrant shade of green than she was used to seeing. Nearby, there were sparse trees strewn with vines, and a shallow pool of murky water, more like a huge puddle than a lake.

Bobbie's boots made a squelching sound. "It's certainly wet here," she said.

"I take you to all the nicest places, don't I?" said Ben. "We should be right on the edge of the swamp now. In the middle of the night, which is good for Jubilant Johnny over there, but not great for us." He swiped at a vine with his sword. "Have your weapon ready. We could run into trouble pretty quickly."

Bobbie did as he suggested, switching the lead to her off hand and gripping her sword with her right. She looked briefly from her gleaming iron sword to Ben's sorry stone version.

"I've been wondering about something," she said, considering her words carefully. She was never entirely sure what would set Ben off. He seemed to have a lot of sore points. "You've been adventuring for a while now, right? So, why don't you have better gear?"

"I did have better gear," he answered. "Some pretty great stuff, in fact. But shortly before I met you, I . . . lost it."

"That seems careless," said Bobbie.

"I took precautions," Ben argued. "But everything was stolen from me. By someone I trusted, actually."

"Oh," said Bobbie. "I'm sorry. That's hard."

"Yeah," said Ben. "Thanks."

"Although . . ."

"Oh, please don't," said Ben.

"Please don't what?"

"Please don't turn this into one of your big-sister teachable moments," he said.

"I don't do that," Bobbie objected, which earned a raised eyebrow. "I don't! I just thought it was worth pointing out that your reaction to getting looted was apparently to come to Plaintown so *you* could loot *us*. So *maybe* it's worth examining whether you think this cycle of plundering is a problem and, if so, whether your actions are partially responsible for perpetuating the cycle."

Ben groaned, and Johnny echoed him. "Hey, I think I understand why he makes that noise now," said Ben. "He's totally exasperated by you!"

"So rude," said Bobbie. "I hope we run into the wild wolves that raised you so that I can ask them where they went wrong."

As they walked, the ground became more sodden, and the trees grew closer together. Soon it was hard to see the moon past the towering trunks and their dense, hanging foliage.

"I've never seen trees like these before," said Bobbie, and she pressed a hand to one as they passed.

"They're mangroves," Ben explained. "They grow big and strong around water." He took another step and was suddenly up to his knees in swamp water. "Ick," he said. "I prefer solid ground, myself."

Johnny growled, which itself wasn't unusual, but this time, the timbre of it was different. It sent prickles down Bobbie's back; it sounded, somehow, like a warning.

She raised her sword and turned to peer into the shadows beneath the trees.

She saw a light, wavering and watery—a green luminescence that she took, at first, as some sort of otherworldly flame. She'd heard stories of ghost lights haunting the Overworld's mires, luring unwary travelers to a mucky, drowning doom. But she'd been certain those were just spooky stories, meant to dissuade young villagers from leaving the safety of their homes. She rubbed her eyes, blinked furiously, and looked again.

She saw now that it was no ghostly light, but instead a quivering, gelatinous mass. Its wet surface reflected the moonlight so that it almost appeared lit from within. It was a sickly shade of green, and as it propelled itself forward with a bouncing motion, Bobbie could see the shadowy impression of a face on its otherwise inhuman form.

"It's cute!" she said, lowering her sword.

"Sure. Cute," said Ben. "Too bad it's a malevolent ball of slime intent on destroying us."

Bobbie smirked. "You said that about the llamas, too."

"Llamas are jerks, and everyone knows it!" Ben said hotly. He stepped between Bobbie and the slime, brandishing his sword. "I'm starting to question your judgment."

Ben waited until the slime took one more quivering leap forward, then he slashed out with his sword. The slime, caught midleap, was an easy target.

But it did not fall to Ben's sword. Instead, it split apart, forming two separate slimes, each half the size of the original.

"I'm questioning *your* judgment," Bobbie said, lifting her sword again. "Because now there are two of them!" *And they're even cuter at that size*, she thought but did not say.

She stood shoulder-to-shoulder with Ben, waiting to see if the slimes would press the attack. "Should we retreat?" she asked.

"It's too dark out here," he said. "And there are way worse things than slimes. The last thing we want is to run into another threat while we still have slimes at our back."

"Okay," said Bobbie. "Then I've got the one on the left."

Bobbie had been paying attention. Just as Ben had before, she waited for the slime to make its move, and she caught it mid-leap. To her consternation, it split in half *again*.

"This is ridiculous!" she said.

To her right, Ben was having the same issue. "Still think they're cute?"

"I mean, kind of," she said. "Now they're pocket-size."

"Just smite them, please," said Ben.

"*Smite* them?" she echoed. "Do adventurers actually talk like that?"

Despite her teasing, Bobbie prepared to do as Ben had suggested—when Johnny leaped suddenly forward, gobbling up one of the tiny slimes in a single gulp.

"Uh," said Bobbie, stopping in her tracks.

"Ew," said Ben. "That *can't* be healthy."

Johnny made a gurgling noise, and Bobbie decided they should take care of the remaining slimes before her brother tried to help himself to seconds.

"Smite!" she said, thwacking the dirt with her sword. The remaining slimes were so small that they made for difficult targets. "Come on, Ben, smite, smite!"

"I'm smiting!" he said, laughing.

Johnny watched them as they slashed at the tiny, hopping mobs, and he released a somewhat slimy burp.

CHAPTER 17

The swamp was still and silent, except for the frogs moving just outside of their reach. Ben took a moment to enjoy their frenetic hopping; he rarely had a reason to pass through a swamp, and he'd never seen the amphibians anywhere else.

Bobbie seemed charmed by them, too. Even her slobbering sibling stood transfixed by the sight.

Which was good, because it kept the young zombie from rocking the boat—literally.

After their slime smiting, Ben had directed Bobbie to collect the slimeballs left behind—"You never know what might come in handy later," he'd told her sagely, and he was *pretty* certain she appreciated the advice, even though she made a face at him. While she gathered the goods and kept Jaundiced Johnny off his back, Ben had hacked into a mangrove to collect the wood he needed to construct a small rowboat.

Then he realized that one of them was a murderous zombie, and he gathered enough wood to craft a *second* boat.

"I don't see why we're in separate boats," Bobbie called from across the water. "Weren't you worried about getting separated?"

"I'm worried about a lot of things," Ben answered. "Getting my nose bitten off by your brother is pretty high on the list."

Bobbie sighed. "He's probably full after eating that slime," she said, as if that would make Ben feel any less concerned about the boy's appetites.

It was in the heart of the swamp that Ben saw what he'd hoped—and dreaded—to see. The trees fell away, and the draping vines parted, and then a rickety structure loomed before them, rising out of the water on tall, wooden stilts. In the moonlight, it looked like some strange, boxy animal standing on legs too thin to reasonably support its weight.

"There," Ben whispered, hoping he could be heard by Bobbie and no one else. "That's a swamp hut. There should be a witch inside."

"I hope they're feeling helpful," said Bobbie. "I'd hate to be turned into a frog or something."

"Oh, don't worry about that," said Ben. "They'd probably just outright kill us . . ."

Bobbie chuckled weakly. "And you think I'll be able to reason with them?"

"I don't know about *reasoning* with them," said Ben. "But I hope you'll be able to communicate with them, at least." He shrugged. "I admit, it's a long shot. I've encountered a couple of witches in the past, and I couldn't make sense of anything they said. But that was true of the wandering trader, too, and you were chatting them up without any problem."

"And witches know all about potions, right?" Bobbie asked.

"All I can say for sure is that, on two different occasions, a witch has thrown a potion at my face." He smirked. "If it happens a third time, I'm going to start wondering if *I'm* the problem."

"You're the problem," Bobbie deadpanned.

Ben ignored her jab. "So, how do you want to do this?" he asked her.

"I don't know," said Bobbie. "I figured I'd just ask politely for information."

Ben frowned. "Sure. After we sneak into the witch's hut, knock them out, and tie them to a chair, right?"

"What? No!" Bobbie was obviously appalled by the thought. "Why would they tell us anything after we invade their home and threaten them?"

"Because our threats will be very convincing . . . ?"

"Adventurers! Honestly," said Bobbie. "You can't just go around acting as if you're entitled to everything!"

"Please stop yelling," said Ben.

Bobbie appeared immediately remorseful. "Ben, I'm sorry, I—I didn't mean to hurt your feelings, I just—"

"I wasn't worried about my feelings," Ben said in a low voice. "I was worried you were being too loud . . ."

It was at that moment that a wicked cackle rang out across the water.

Ben's gaze snapped up to the hut, where a figure had appeared in the open doorway. The figure resembled a villager but wore a peaked hat and flowing purple robes. Despite being the source of the raucous laughter, they did not seem especially good-natured.

"Witch!" he said, pointing.

"Yes, thank you, I see them," Bobbie sang. Then, raising her voice: "Hello, kindly witch, mage of the mire, bruja of brewing, esteemed wise-person of the wilderness . . ."

The witch hefted a splash potion in their grip, and Ben gestured for Bobbie to get to the point already.

"Ahem. We are here on a quest and seek your aid," she said. "You see, my brother has been transformed, and I was hoping you may know of a cure—or that you might be able to invent one."

The witch paced up and down the porch of the hut, waving a flask around and yapping unintelligibly.

"Oh, no," said Bobbie. "I . . . I can't understand what they're saying." She turned to Ben. "They almost sound like a villager, but not quite. I think I'm picking up on some hostility, though . . ."

"You think so?" said Ben. "Hostility, you said?"

With a sharp cackle, the witch hurled the flask at Bobbie. "Duck!" said Ben, but Bobbie didn't listen. She took the full brunt of the splash potion as the flask shattered against her.

"Hey, that hurt!" said Bobbie.

"Why didn't you duck?" cried Ben.

"My baby brother is right behind me," said Bobbie. "I couldn't let *him* get hit."

"I've never been so glad to be an only child," muttered Ben, and he paddled out in front of Bobbie. "Hey! Witchy!" he cried, waving his arms. "Why don't you aim over here instead?"

"What are you doing?" Bobbie asked him over the witch's madcap cackling.

"I have a shield. I'll be fine!" he told her. "You sneak around back and build a staircase up to the porch."

"And then what do I do?" Bobbie asked, already paddling away.

Ben met an oncoming potion with his shield. It shattered, and he batted the lingering fumes away.

"Try asking politely one more time," said Ben.

"Really?" said Bobbie.

"No!" he said. "Hit them over the head with something heavy! Or sic that nightmare you call a brother on them!"

"That was a rude thing to say, and we will discuss it later!" Bobbie called as she paddled around the far side of the hut. Ben, through a combination of taunts, gestures, and experimental dance moves, managed to keep the witch's attention on him.

As he dodged a fifth potion, Ben began to wonder when Bobbie would make her dramatic entrance. He kept expecting to see her sword poking through the witch; or perhaps Johnny would tackle the mob, sailing over the edge of the balcony and dragging the witch into the murky water below. Ben would have a perfect view of whatever ending befell their witchy adversary.

As he dodged a *sixth* potion, he called up in a singsong voice, "What is taking so long up there?"

"We're done!" said Bobbie, and her voice was *not* coming from above. She reappeared from around the far side of the stilts, rowing her boat toward Ben, Johnny gnawing absentmindedly on a bone.

"What do you mean you're done?" said Ben, and, distracted, he ducked a thrown potion just in time. "I thought you were going to smite the witch?"

"It's always smiting with you," Bobbie said, and she smiled. "I went through the witch's things. Found a recipe book with different formulas than Cleric Avery had. Maybe there's something in here we can use."

"And where did the bone come from?" Ben asked, a little bit afraid of the answer.

"Oh. That was just lying on the floorboards," said Bobbie.

"Is that sanitary?" asked Ben.

"Well, he *wanted* to eat the cat," said Bobbie. "So this felt like a good compromise."

Ben sighed. "I guess zombies probably don't have to worry about germs," he said, then he turned his head up toward the witch. "You don't know how lucky you are! If it had been me up there, you'd have been smited! Or . . . smote?"

"I'm sorry about the burglary," Bobbie called up to the witch as she rowed past Ben and back toward shore. "I want to break the callous cycle of looting, so I'll try to find a way to get your book back to you one day."

As Ben rowed after her, he called over his shoulder, "But we're keeping the bone!"

CHAPTER 18

The sun threatened to rise at any moment, and Johnny put up a fuss when Bobbie tried to put the pumpkin on his head, so Ben suggested they set up camp as soon as they had put a little distance between themselves and the witch.

"This spot should be fine," Ben said, and he brought his pickaxe to bear against a low, soggy hill on the outskirts of the swamp. Within seconds, he had carved out a small space just below ground level, with a torch for light and room for beds and crafting stations, in case they decided to stay there for the day.

Bobbie sat beneath the torch and set immediately to examining the book she'd stolen. "It's not *completely* coherent," said Bobbie. "It's mostly scribbles and drawings. But I can interpret some of it. Especially the opening pages." She held it up for Ben to see. "Look at this first entry."

Ben leaned in for a look, but as soon as he got close, Johnny growled menacingly. "Why don't you summarize it for me?" he suggested.

Bobbie nodded. "Well, from what I can tell, the witch wasn't always a witch. They were a village cleric, and they used this book to record their experiments." She flipped through the pages. "Something happened. A storm? A bolt of lightning? It transformed them." She looked at her brother, tied to his wooden post. "Sort of like Johnny, in a way," she said sadly.

"Keep reading," said Ben. "I'll check our gear, maybe patch things up and make some more torches. You hungry?"

Bobbie frowned. "I don't think I can eat until we're clear of the swamp. It smells funny in here."

"Yeah," Ben agreed. "Now that you mention it, it smells sort of like rotting flesh. Hmm. I wonder what that could be?"

Bobbie sniffed the air, then grimaced. "All the more reason to find a cure," she said, and she turned back to the book in her lap.

It was sometime later, and Ben was gnawing on a loaf of semi-stale bread when Bobbie hopped suddenly to her feet. "It's here. It's actually here!" She looked over at Ben, a huge smile spreading across her face. "The witch must have been looking for a cure for their own condition. They were documenting cures for all sorts of things—everything from poisoning and bad-luck curses to *zombification*." She passed him the book, opened to a page with a hand-drawn illustration.

He recognized the image immediately. "That's a golden apple," he said.

"It's a real thing?" Bobbie asked. "It exists?"

"Yeah," said Ben. "They exist. They're even craftable."

Bobbie took the book back and flipped to the next page. "We need one. If I understand this right, a golden apple—when combined with the effects of a Potion of Weakness—will *cure* Johnny. Completely and forever." Tears welled in Bobbie's eyes. "I knew it was possible. I just knew it."

"I guess I shouldn't have doubted you," Ben said.

"That's right," said Bobbie, chuckling as she wiped at her cheeks. "Do you . . . are you a hugger?" she asked. "I think I'd like a hug."

"Sure," said Ben, and he stepped toward her, then stopped short when Johnny growled and pulled at his lead. "Uh, or not," said Ben. "Maybe later?"

Bobbie nodded, her tears gone. "Tell you what," she said. "If you can tell me how to craft a golden apple, that will count as a dozen hugs in one."

"It's a simple recipe, but it would take a long time to get our hands on enough gold," Ben replied. "We might have better luck trying to find one. My buddy, Logan, found one once."

"Do you know where Logan is now?"

"Well, no," Ben said, and he felt a little pang. "And anyway, he ate that one. He said it was the most delicious thing he'd ever tasted, but I had to take his word for it. He did tell me where he'd found it, though. Hold on a minute."

Ben rummaged through his things, pulling out the maps he'd taken from the two cartographers' houses. He flipped through them, laying them out on the floor, searching for something he'd spotted earlier.

"There," he said, pointing to a small rectangle in the heart of a forest. "A woodland mansion." He looked up at Bobbie. "It's not a sure thing. But you can sometimes find golden apples there."

"A mansion, like in the storybooks?" Bobbie swooned. "Is the family who lives there nice? Do they want nothing more than to share their bounty of gold-plated fruits and vegetables with well-traveled strangers?"

"Yeah, it's sort of like that, except the complete opposite." Ben shook his head. "I'd better take another look at our gear, and you should get some sleep. Because we're in for a very tough fight."

This time, when Bobbie failed to take his advice, Ben knew better than to take it personally. He'd told her to get some sleep, and he knew that she'd tried. But she was too anxious about their plan — too eager to get her brother back to normal. She lay in bed, but sleep wouldn't take her.

Ben wondered if the fact that Johnny was looming right at the foot of her bed contributed to her insomnia, too.

"He really watches over me when I sleep?" she asked.

"Every time," said Ben. "He won't let me get anywhere near you."

"We've come a long way," said Bobbie. "His first few days as a zombie, he tried to eat me every chance he got." She seemed to consider something. "Hey, come here," she said.

Ben looked up from his crafting table. "No way," he said. "Didn't you just hear me? I get close, he gets bitey."

"Here," Bobbie said, and she tossed an iron boot in his direction. "Put that on your hand." Before he could object, she said, "If you wanted, we could skip the part where you whine about it and get right to the part where you do what I ask you to do."

"You underestimate me," Ben said, taking up the boot. "I can whine *while* I do what you ask me to do. Is my hand going to smell like a foot after this?"

"Johnny, look over there," said Bobbie, and she pointed to a very uninteresting wall of dirt. The zombie boy dutifully turned his head, however, gazing at the dirt as if it held some great secret.

With her brother distracted, Bobbie slipped out of bed,

grabbed Johnny's bone from the floor, and handed it to Ben. He took it with his free hand.

"Great," said Ben. "Now one hand smells like foot, and the other smells like zombie saliva. This bone is awfully wet." He narrowed his eyes at Bobbie. "And that isn't whining. I'm just stating a fact!"

At the sound of Ben's voice, Johnny turned, a low growl in his throat. He took a few steps toward them before the lead stopped him short.

"Okay," said Bobbie. "I want you to get into his range. Offer him the bone."

"And what if he ignores the bone and goes after me?" asked Ben.

"That's fine," said Bobbie. "He can't chew through iron, and he can't maneuver very much when he's tied to his post. Keep your armored hand up in front of you, and you'll be okay."

Ben crept forward with both of his hands raised. "Here you go, Johnny," he cooed. "A nice, slimy chew toy, just for you." He frowned. "To be clear, I'm talking about the bone. *I'm* not slimy."

Johnny ignored Ben's humor—and he ignored the bone. As soon as Ben was in range, the zombie attempted to bite him. As Bobbie had predicted, however, the boy's teeth couldn't penetrate the makeshift gauntlet.

It didn't stop him from trying, though. Johnny kept his mouth affixed to the boot, gnawing and drooling in equal measure.

"What's he even doing?" Ben said.

"He's *learning*," Bobbie said. "Eventually, he'll figure out that trying to bite you only gets him a mouthful of bland iron . . . and that he'll be much happier going for the bone."

"Eventually," echoed Ben. "How long will this take?"

"Well, for me, it took a few hours . . ."

"That isn't too bad," said Ben.

"A few hours *every day*," Bobbie clarified. "For . . . many days in a row . . ."

Ben looked at Johnny, who still gnawed away futilely. "I guess we all learn at our own pace," he said, sighing. But then he had an idea. "So how about I give *you* a lesson now?"

Bobbie seemed wary. "What do you want to teach me?"

"So many things!" Ben said. He smirked at her. "But let's start with combat."

CHAPTER 19

"**S**o you've heard all about these mansions, but you've never seen one yourself?" Bobbie asked him, as they traveled across the Overworld by the light of the moon.

"I actually *did* see one once," Ben told her. "From the outside, at a safe distance. I'd heard all sorts of stories about what might be stalking around inside, and I figured I wasn't ready for that sort of challenge." He looked up at the moon. "That was before I met Logan. He really helped me refine my skills. I'm ready for a woodland mansion now." He hoped.

They had left the swamp behind them and were traveling back through the savanna region surrounding Savannaton. It was warm, like the swamp, but without all the murky water. Ben was relieved not to have to devote so much mental energy to watching his step—particularly since they needed to be on the lookout for hostile creatures.

For once, they weren't trying to avoid dangerous mobs. In fact, Ben was hoping to find a bit of trouble.

It didn't take long. The trees here were sparse, giving them a good view of their surroundings, and in the dead of night, monsters were never hard to come by.

"I see something," whispered Bobbie. "To the northwest."

Ben strained his eyes, peering into the dark, then nodded. "It's a creeper. That's perfect."

"You have a weird definition of 'perfect,'" said Bobbie. "Aren't creepers the ones who blow up?"

"When you get close, yeah," said Ben. He ducked behind a tree and gestured for her to do the same. "That means the timing of your attacks is critical. And that's the exact lesson you need to learn."

Bobbie looked over her shoulder at him as she tied her brother's lead to a post. "My timing was pretty good against that spider in Savannaton."

"Yeah, but I was drawing its attention with my . . . strategic weeping," Ben said. "What about the siege on your village? Did you fight any zombies that night?"

"Sort of," Bobbie answered. "But I didn't defeat any. I would hit one and then run before it could recover."

"That's what I'm talking about," said Ben. "It's easy enough to hit an enemy one time. But when a mob is coming after you— when it's actually fighting back—you need to choose your moments carefully. Just slashing out randomly will leave you open to a counterattack."

"Like with the slimes," said Bobbie. "The way you waited until they were leaping forward."

"Exactly," said Ben. "It's even more important with a creeper. You have an iron sword, which means it'll take several hits to defeat it. If you just stand in place and slash, you're in big trouble."

"Kaboom?" asked Bobbie.

"Kaboom," Ben confirmed. "Focus on your footwork—keep some distance between you, then dart forward and slash when you see an opening."

Bobbie hefted her sword. She had a good grip, but Ben could see the doubt in her eyes. "You've got this," he said. "You're smart, and that's what wins a fight." He thought about that for a second. "Sometimes a diamond sword wins a fight. But we work with what we have."

As they approached the creeper, Ben let Bobbie walk ahead of him. He kept close, though, and had his sword at the ready. If her timing was off—if she got into trouble—he would have only seconds to step in and help her.

But he needn't have worried. Bobbie was a natural. Once the creeper had noticed her, she held her ground, letting it come to her . . . then batting it away with her sword as soon as it had come within reach. She did just as Ben told her, keeping her sword up as she stepped back, then lunging forward to attack.

Bobbie leaped up and cheered when the creeper at last fell over and evaporated in a burst of harmless dust. Ben wanted to cheer with her, but he shushed her instead. "You don't want to draw every hostile mob in the area this way," he warned. "Beating a mob in one-on-one combat is one thing, but fighting multiple enemies?"

"You're as stingy with your praise as you are with your loot," said Bobbie, and she ran forward to collect the small pile of gunpowder left behind by the creeper. "So I'm keeping this!"

Ben laughed. "Fair. But be careful with it. That isn't food seasoning, you know."

They went back to collect Johnny, then continued on their way. Bobbie, still feeling the rush of battle, scanned the horizon for their next adversary. "What's that?" she said. "In the distance. Over there."

Ben turned to look—then quickly averted his eyes. His brief glimpse was enough to give the impression of a tall, spindly figure, unnaturally long in the limbs and with eyes that glowed violet in the dark.

"That's an Enderman," he said. "Don't look."

They crouched behind a small incline. They were still a good distance from the mob, but their route would take them right past it.

"I've seen one of them before," Bobbie told him. "It was eerie but seemed harmless."

"They *are* harmless, usually. But they can also be very aggressive," Ben explained. "Staring at them is a surefire way to set them off. And they're tricky to fight, so I'd rather avoid angering it. Let's just hang here for a minute and hope it goes about its business."

"Okay," Bobbie said, but she began fidgeting almost immediately. "It's *hard* not to look, though," she said. "It's like when someone tells you not to think about axolotls, and then that's all you can think about for the rest of the day."

"That sounds like a very strange game," said Ben. "But I know what you mean. By not looking at the Enderman, you don't know what it's doing, and so it feels like you're vulnerable to an attack. But the Enderman only attacks *if* you look at it. It's like a mind game. You've just got to exert control over your own impulses, and—oh no." Ben turned to look at Johnny, who stood off to the side, gazing out into the night. "Zombie boy over there is nothing *but* impulses."

"Johnny," said Bobbie. "Yoo-hoo! Look at me. Don't look out there." At his complete lack of response, she just shook her head.

"Well, I never could get him to listen." She sat in silence for a moment, then turned back to Ben. "How much of him is still . . . in there, do you think? When we cure him, will he remember any of this?"

"I have no idea," said Ben, and he leaned against the grassy hillock at his back. "I mean, how much do *you* remember about being a baby? We tend to forget all sorts of things."

"I don't remember much," Bobbie agreed.

Ben hesitated before he pressed on. "So you . . . Have you always lived in Plaintown?" he asked. "You're, I mean, *from* there?"

"I know what you're getting at," said Bobbie. "I used to get questions like that whenever an adventurer passed through town."

"I don't mean to pry—"

"No, it's okay," Bobbie said. "I'm not sensitive about it. I'm obviously *different* from most villagers." She shrugged. "I'm adopted. My parents found me as a baby. And, to answer your earlier question, I don't remember that day or anything before it. Growing up, I always knew I was a foundling—they never hid that from me—but they've always been my parents, as far back as I remember." She looked suddenly solemn. "Or, they *were* my parents. I keep forgetting they're not back home waiting for me."

Ben wasn't entirely comfortable with displays of emotion, but he knew better than to let those words hang in the air unacknowledged. "I'm sorry," he said; then, after a moment's hesitation, he reached over and patted her on her helmet.

Bobbie gave him a puzzled look. "Did you just pet me?"

"No, I—I was comforting you," he answered.

"Is that what that was?" Bobbie said, and she laughed. "But, hey! Johnny didn't bite your hand off or anything. That's progress."

"Yeah," said Ben. "He and I will be best buddies in no time, I bet."

Johnny, sensing their renewed attention, made a ghastly, rasping noise.

"Adorable," said Ben, and he peeked out from above the incline. "All clear, I think. And Johnny didn't draw the Enderman's ire, so maybe things are really starting to go our way."

"Knock on wood," said Bobbie, and she set down a wooden plank, just so she had something to hit as she said it.

CHAPTER 20

Even Johnny seemed wary to walk among the trees of the dark forest. Bobbie sensed the slightest hesitation on his part, a subtle tug upon his lead as they approached the tree line, as if he were dragging his feet.

She wanted to give him a pep talk. But as the dark oak trees loomed before them and the inky blackness of tree-shrouded night opened to receive them, it was all she could do to suppress a shudder of fear.

She'd almost gotten used to the darkness of night. But the forest offered a deeper darkness, its thick canopy of leaves blocking out any hint of the moonlight.

"This is creepy," Bobbie whispered as they entered the forest. "But . . . nothing to worry about, right?"

"Oh, there's a *lot* to worry about," said Ben. "Keep your eyes open—this place is probably crawling with monsters."

The trees grew close together, so they had to walk single file instead of side-by-side. Bobbie let Ben walk in front so that she could remain between him and Johnny.

"It isn't much farther," Ben said, consulting the map. "We might actually make it there without any hassle."

Bobbie knew as soon as he said it that they were doomed.

There was a *twang* sound, and a rush of air, and suddenly the tree next to Ben appeared to sprout a new limb.

Not a limb, Bobbie realized. An *arrow*.

"We're under attack!" she yelled, and Ben told her, "Run!"

She did as he suggested, happily—but there were so many trees, and it was so dark. She made it only a few steps before Johnny's lead became tangled, wrapped around a trunk they'd passed on opposite sides.

The fastest way to untangle him was to drop the lead. But she worried too much about getting separated in the forest. It would be too easy for him to disappear into the gloom.

But maybe that gloom would work to their advantage. Maybe they'd already evaded their attacker.

No such luck. Bobbie looked back in the direction they'd fled from. She could see movement in the gloom—a shock of white, a ghoulish face, and a bow, aimed directly at her.

Before Bobbie could react, Ben was there, stepping in front of her and batting the arrow aside with his shield.

"Wow, thanks," said Bobbie.

"I'd say don't mention it, but I live for the praise," said Ben, and he ran ahead, closing the distance between him and the attacker in four quick strides. Bobbie watched to be certain he had the upper hand before she turned away and set to untangling Johnny's lead. For his part, her brother simply stood in place, blinking.

"One skeleton down," said Ben. "I got some more arrows from it. And look. It's fresh!" He held a bone out to Johnny, who sniffed it with suspicion before snatching it from Ben's grip. He sat down in the dirt and set immediately to gnawing on it.

"You know, that's still creepy," said Ben.

"I'm sorry," said Bobbie. "I was no help at all."

"Oh, I wouldn't say that," Ben said. "You drew its fire long enough for me to get into striking distance." He hefted his sword, which appeared blunted with overuse. "I still wish I had a better blade, though. It took forever to hack it up, and we're making too much noise. I have a feeling we're about to be overwhelmed."

"What can we do?" asked Bobbie. "Should we try to tunnel the rest of the way?"

"Right idea, wrong direction." Ben smirked. "You're not afraid of heights, are you?"

Bobbie hadn't thought she was afraid of heights. But she'd never really put that to the test.

"Are you sure these things can support our weight?" she asked, holding out her arms to steady herself.

"Pretty sure," Ben answered. "As long as you don't make a wrong step."

Bobbie gripped the lead more tightly. "Stay close, Johnny," she said. "Step where I step."

Johnny, gnawing on his bone, made no reply.

They had taken to the canopy, crossing the breadth of the forest by way of its verdant rooftop. Shadowy shapes lurked far below them—Bobbie caught glimpses of them through the leaves—but up top, there were no mobs or monsters for her to fear. Only gravity, and the gentle sway of the branches beneath their feet.

She moved slowly but steadily, taking one measured step at a time.

Despite its size, the woodland mansion seemed to Bobbie to almost appear out of nowhere. One moment, she was navigating the endless expanse of canopy. The next, the leaves parted, and she saw the great building looming before them.

It was huge. Perhaps as large as all of Plaintown. Built of dark wood and cobblestone, it rose above the trees like a massive beast, its rows of identical windows glaring out like the eyes of a spider— pitiless, multitudinous points of light in the dark.

Bobbie followed Ben's careful hop from canopy to eaves, then guided Johnny across the small gap. They stood together on a sloping roof of wood, similar to the oak used to construct Plaintown, but darker. "Which way's the front door?" asked Bobbie. "And how are we getting down from here?"

"You have got to stop thinking like a villager," said Ben. And with his sword, he shattered the nearest window. "Ta-da! One entrance."

Bobbie gasped. "That's hardly going to endear us to whoever lives here!"

"We're not here to make friends, Bobbie," Ben said as he ducked through the window frame. "And the creeps who call this place home were *never* going to like us."

Bobbie followed him inside, pulling Johnny in behind her. They were in some kind of dining room, with potted flowers placed atop a long table and simple chandeliers hanging from the ceiling. Nearly everything was made of wood.

"It's sort of cozy," Bobbie said, determined to be positive. The truth was, the house had an unsettling atmosphere.

Ben affected a spooky voice. "If you like it here, then perhaps you will stay . . . forever!" He waved his hands in front of her face and made ghostly noises.

She slapped his hands away. "You're not funny. Or scary. Or whatever it is you're trying to be!"

"Charming," said Ben, pretending to pout. "The answer is always charming."

"Then you're way off the mark," teased Bobbie.

"I won *him* over," said Ben. But Johnny, having completely devoured the bone that had been occupying his attention, growled menacingly in Ben's direction. "That beastly growl reminds me — we should be careful. These places are supposed to be *crawling* with trouble. Not just monsters, but spellcasters and axe murderers, too."

Bobbie barely suppressed a shudder. "I was picturing a bright palace out of a fairy tale. But this is more like a haunted house from a ghost story."

"There's no such thing as ghosts," said Ben. "Worry about the axe murderers instead."

They moved quietly, swords drawn as they crept into the upstairs hallway. The hall was high-ceilinged, with tall columns, and lined with torches and open doors. A vibrant red carpet ran the length of the hall; looking at it, Bobbie tried not to be reminded of blood.

It was only a short distance to the first open doorway, which Ben approached with caution. He leaned against the hallway wall for a moment, gripping his sword in front of him and taking a deep breath before he whirled around, rushing into the room in a battle-ready stance. Only a moment later, he said, "It's all clear. And . . . sort of random."

Bobbie saw what he meant as soon as she followed him inside. It was a small, boxy room, empty of threat — empty of everything, except for a large pile of wool, all dyed various shades of blue.

"On the long list of things I was expecting to see," said Bobbie, "blue wool was *very* low."

Johnny's reaction was somewhat more enthusiastic. The zombie boy groaned, lurched forward, and fell face-first into the pile of wool.

"Did he do that on purpose?" asked Ben. "He's not going to *eat* it, is he?"

Bobbie watched as her brother thrashed around, sending blocks of wool flying in the air and across the room. She smiled, a little sadly. "He's playing," she said. "See? He *is* still in there, somewhere."

The next room contained rows of bookshelves and inviting benches; it made Bobbie immediately nostalgic for Plaintown's library—and a little guilty, remembering the state she'd left it in. After that, they found a bedroom with a neatly made bed. The musty air suggested to Bobbie that the room had not been used in some time.

They relaxed their guard as they continued exploring room after room. Bobbie, for one, assumed that the place must be completely abandoned. Ben was a little more wary, but even he let his sword fall to his side.

"This is outright bizarre," Bobbie said as she examined an oak tree growing from a small patch of dirt. "Who puts a tree inside a house?"

Ben crouched beside her, checking a chest for traps. "Slimeballs," he said once he'd finally opened it. "It's empty. And look." He stood, crossing to the room's entrance. "At some point, this room was sealed off with planks. The 'door' we came through is actually a hole that somebody made." He shook his head. "That explains the lack of monsters. Somebody's come through and cleared them all out."

"You say that like it's a bad thing," said Bobbie. "But I could use fewer monsters in my life."

"You don't get it," said Ben. "It's a high-risk, high-reward situation. These mansions are supposed to be perilous, but adventurers still seek them out because the loot makes it worth the danger."

"Loot like . . . a golden apple?" asked Bobbie.

"Yeah. Exactly." Ben sighed. "Someone beat us here. They picked the place clean of anything valuable. We won't find a golden apple here."

Bobbie fought a wave of disappointment—*again*. She struggled not to let her frustration show; instead, she forced a smile. "Well, we'll just have to look somewhere else," she said. "Let's come up with a new plan."

Ben, confronted with her optimism, responded—with a look of abject terror.

Bobbie, perplexed, said, "Are you okay with that? We can renegotiate your rate, if it helps."

Ben gripped her by the shoulders and whirled her around. At the far end of the hallway, she saw what had him so frightened.

"Is that a—?" she began.

"G-g-ghost!" said Ben.

CHAPTER 21

The ghostly creature hadn't seen them yet. It drifted aimlessly along the hallway on dark, tattered wings. As Ben watched, it passed right through a column, as if it had no physical substance.

But the sword it held looked substantive enough to do some damage.

"I thought there were *no such things* as ghosts," hissed Bobbie.

"Believe me, so did I," whispered Ben. "I've definitely never seen one before now. But it doesn't look too tough. I mean, it's got a sword, which is better than barbed tentacles or a prehensile ectoplasmic tongue."

"Your imagination is horrible," said Bobbie.

They stood in silence for a moment, considering the specter at a distance. "Okay, here's what we're going to do," Ben said at last. "I'm going to try to take it out from here with arrows. You be ready with your sword in case the arrows don't do enough damage."

"Are you sure it's hostile?" asked Bobbie.

Ben wasted no time swapping his sword for a bow and lining up his shot. "If it's not hostile now, it's about to be." He let the arrow fly.

It *thunk*ed harmlessly into a column, missing its target by a good margin.

"What was that?" asked Bobbie.

"I'm out of practice," said Ben. "Sword, sword!"

The arrow had failed to hit, but it had succeeded in drawing the mob's attention. It flapped its wings furiously, bearing down on them with sinister intent in its eyes.

Johnny leaped into its path, knocking it off course before it got close enough to swing its sword. With the mob caught off guard, Ben and Bobbie acted quickly, attacking in unison. Ben worried their weapons might pass right through it, but his fears were unfounded. The mob was vanquished in a matter of moments.

"That went well," said Ben. "Maybe that should have been the plan all along."

"We're not done yet," warned Bobbie. And Ben lifted his gaze in time to see that a second ghostly imp had materialized at the very end of the hallway.

"How many arrows do you have?" asked Bobbie.

"Not enough," said Ben. "Let's just stab it a whole bunch!"

Ben ran down the remaining stretch of red carpet, striking the mob with his sword before it could react to his presence. After that first blow, he stood back, lifting his shield and staying out of its reach while he learned its attack patterns. In the meantime, Bobbie snuck around behind it. Trapped between them, the mob proved easy prey.

"Did you see where it came from?" Ben asked. "Did it just appear out of nowhere?"

"Not nowhere," said Bobbie, and she pressed a hand to the wall. "It came right through this wall. But there's no door."

"Well . . ." said Ben.

"I know." Bobbie smirked, put her sword away, and pulled out a pickaxe. "I need to stop thinking like a villager, right?"

As soon as Bobbie had made an opening, Ben ran through it with his sword held high. Whatever might be on the other side of the wall, he had a feeling that the element of surprise would be crucial.

But Ben hesitated when he saw a *figure* inside. They looked at Ben with wide eyes, uttering a startled sound, and then raised their hands. Ben saw immediately that those hands were empty of any weapons.

Had this stranger been trapped here, in a small, dark room? Did they need help?

"Uh, hi!" said Ben, lowering his sword. "Everything cool in here? Sorry to barge in . . ."

The stranger's face twisted in an unmistakable sign of aggression. Ben had the sudden impression that their arms were not raised in surrender after all—that those empty hands were calling forth some terrible power.

"Slimeballs—he's casting a spell," Ben said under his breath. He charged—

Too late. With a word of command—it sounded like "wololo"—the spellcaster summoned a ring of traps, one of which appeared just beneath Ben's feet. It snapped shut, like a mouth lined with razor-sharp fangs, and Ben was pinned in place. The pain was excruciating—like being stabbed with a half dozen swords all at once.

Through the haze of pain, Ben chided himself for dropping

his guard. It was Bobbie's fault—she had rubbed off on him, in the worst possible way. And now her talk-first-fight-later approach was going to get him killed.

An arrow whizzed by his ear, lodging itself in the spellcaster's shoulder. They barked in pain and surprise, then turned to flee.

The trap released its grip on Ben, and he staggered to the floor. "Nice shot," he said through teeth clenched in pain.

"Thanks," said Bobbie. "I just tried to do the opposite of what you did. So far it's working out for me."

"Happy to help," wheezed Ben, and he rose unsteadily to his feet. The spellcaster—Ben recognized it now as an evoker—was a dangerous foe, but wearing only a simple robe, they were also a *vulnerable* one. The evoker was attempting to escape, but there was no other exit from the room. Ben and Bobbie had them cornered.

This time, Ben showed no mercy. With the wicked wizard backed up against a wall, he brought his sword down, while Bobbie continued firing arrows from a distance. Their foe finally collapsed, then turned to dust.

"They dropped some loot," Ben said, but he sat back on the floor. "Grab it, would you? I need to eat something to get my strength back."

While Ben munched on a slice of melon, Bobbie bent to retrieve the unfamiliar item. "It's some kind of doll," she said. "It's familiar, but from where?" She held it out for Ben to see. It was a golden idol, humanoid in shape, with bright green eyes.

"I've never seen anything like it," he said.

Johnny, whose lead Bobbie had dropped in the commotion, wandered over to sniff at the item. Evidently deciding it was inedible, he wandered off again.

"Hold on," said Bobbie, and she stashed the idol in her inventory, then pulled out the witch's journal and began flipping through it. "Aha!" she said, tapping at the open page. "It's in here. It's some sort of magic relic. There's a picture of a skull with an X drawn over it." She looked up at Ben. "Maybe it's a weapon against skeletons?"

"Sounds valuable," Ben said. "Let's hold on to it." He felt his strength returning, but the memory of those fangs was hard to shake. "Who knows what else we're going to run into in this place?"

As it turned out, they didn't encounter any more resistance as they continued to explore the mansion. And, other than a few melons harvested from an indoor farm, they didn't find any loot, either.

"Whoever ransacked the place must have missed that hidden room," Ben said as they stood in the entrance hall on the ground floor. "Other than that, they were impressively thorough."

"So now what?" asked Bobbie. "Do we need to find another forest? Another mansion?"

"That could take a long time," said Ben. "*Years.* I've got another idea."

Ben led them out the front door, onto a cobblestone porch surrounded by dark oak trees. The canopy extended right up to the mansion's walls, and though it was day, the shade was deep and unbroken, protecting Johnny from direct sunlight.

A pop of red caught Ben's eye, standing out against the otherwise muted colors of the mansion's exterior. Someone had planted a banner beside the entrance—a long red flag, emblazoned with the image of a skull and crossbones.

But that wasn't why Ben had led them here. He once more drew his sword, then, straining to reach, he set to slashing through the canopy. The leaves frayed, the branches shattered, and, after a short while, an item dropped from the broken foliage.

Ben leaned over, picked it up, and presented it to Bobbie. It was a perfect, glossy, bright-red apple.

"If we can't find a golden apple," he told her, "then we'll just have to make one."

CHAPTER 22

They needed to go deeper.

"Deeper?" said Bobbie. "I feel like we've been digging for ages."

Just as she'd never had an opportunity to consider whether she was afraid of heights, Bobbie had rarely had occasion to wonder if she might be claustrophobic. She'd done a little digging for coal in the past, and she'd felt no great sense of unease when they had walked the underground rail tunnel or camped out in Ben's burrow on the edge of the swamp.

But this was different. There were blocks upon blocks of dirt hanging suspended over her head, obstructing her access to free and open air. Bobbie tried not to think about it, but that proved as hard as resolving not to look at an Enderman. Her mind kept drifting back to cramped, suffocating thoughts.

Ben kept digging. "Deeper is better," he said. "Technically you can find gold almost anywhere, but it's more common a bit farther down than this."

Ben cut a narrow, descending passage through the subterranean stone, like a steep and artless staircase. At his direction, Bobbie placed torches along their path, and she picked up stray bits of coal that came loose as he dug.

"We make a good team!" she said brightly.

"Sure," he said, huffing. "That's what the person with the easy job *always* says."

"Oops, I just dropped Johnny's lead," Bobbie said.

"What?!" Ben said, and he whirled around, gripping his pickaxe like a sword.

"Just kidding!" Bobbie said brightly. "But let me know if you want to trade jobs at any point."

Ben gave her a dirty look. "I'll stick to digging, thanks."

Eventually, Ben hacked his way through to a cave. Their narrow, descending passage opened up into an underground space about the size of Bobbie's home, but with craggy, irregular edges, and a single passageway that led off into pitch darkness. Bobbie was quick to place torches all around.

"Careful with those," Ben said. "We're in trouble if we run out."

"I've got wood and coal," Bobbie replied. "I can make more if we need them. Which way from here?"

"Well, that's the beauty," said Ben. "There's no wrong answer."

"It kind of sounds like there's no *right* answer."

"There's no guarantee. That's why it's an adventure!" He hefted his pickaxe. "Start digging and see what you find."

Bobbie dug as directed. She didn't find much of anything, though. Andesite . . . diorite . . . granite . . .

Soon her inventory was full of various types of stone.

"Just dump that stuff anywhere," Ben told her.

"What? You mean litter?" Bobbie shook her head. "I'm not really comfortable with that."

"It isn't littering," Ben insisted. "You're just putting it back." He sighed. "You can arrange it artfully if that makes you feel better."

Bobbie began stacking her excess stone in little columns while Johnny tugged lightly on his lead, growling with boredom.

Ben was clearly distracted and unnerved by the noise.

"Growling is usually my first sign that danger's coming," he said. "So he's sort of throwing me off."

"Do you have any more bones for him to gnaw on?" Bobbie asked.

"You're spoiling him," Ben said, and he stomped over to a dark corner of the cavern. He planted a fence post into the ground, then stomped back over to take Johnny's lead.

"Careful," Bobbie said.

"I know," said Ben, and he affixed the lead to the post. "He'll be fine over there. And over *here* . . ." Ben crossed to the opposite side of Bobbie and placed a small chest beneath one of the torches. He'd picked up the chest in Savannaton, promising it would come in handy eventually. "We can keep anything we're not actively using inside this chest. That way we're not littering, and we'll have plenty of room in our inventory for anything exciting we might find."

"Makes sense," said Bobbie. She opened the chest and filled it with stone, coal, wood, and emeralds. She held on to the witch's journal, the seashell, and the strange idol she'd taken from the evoker, plus her iron sword and pickaxe—both of which were beginning to show signs of wear.

She got back to digging immediately after that. More stone,

more coal—and then, a golden glint shone through a slab of gray.

"I think I found some gold!" Bobbie said excitedly.

Ben peered over her shoulder. "No. Sorry," he said. "That's iron."

Bobbie groaned.

"It's super useful!" he said. "Our tools won't last forever, so you want to grab as much iron as you can find."

"If you say so," said Bobbie. She tried not to feel so discouraged, but this was already taking longer than she'd hoped. It was difficult, monotonous work, and the cave was eerie, even after the haunted house. That space, at least, appeared habitable—*meant* for people—with chandeliers and bookshelves and chairs. Underground, she felt like an intruder in a landscape that was not meant for her—a cold, alien place that did not care for her comfort. The silence, in particular, unnerved her.

The silence . . . why *was* it so silent, all of a sudden?

Bobbie poked out of the little hole she'd been digging. She looked over to where Ben had tied Johnny up.

The fence post was right where she remembered it. But her brother was nowhere to be seen.

"Johnny's missing!" she cried.

"Say what?" said Ben, who popped out of his own hole. He saw the empty fence post. "Oh no," he said, and he looked wildly in every direction. "He could be anywhere. He could attack us at any moment!"

Bobbie huffed. "More important—my brother could be lost underground! Forever!"

"Oh, right," Ben said sheepishly. "Yeah. That would also be bad."

CHAPTER 23

"**L**ook on the bright side," Ben said to her as they ran. "As a zombie, your brother is probably safe from monsters. Remember the Enderman? It didn't seem to notice him watching it."

"That's something, I guess," said Bobbie.

"Yeah," said Ben. "The real concern is environmental hazards. He could end up in lava, for instance. Or fall into a chasm or climb out into the sun. Or—oh, this would be bad—what if another adventurer finds him?"

"Ben, stop trying to make me feel better," said Bobbie. "*Please.*"

They were rushing down a naturally formed tunnel of stone. The irregular floor meant that they either had to hop down or jump up every few steps, and Bobbie was having a hard time watching her footing while also checking for side paths and placing torches every dozen blocks or so.

"We're running low on torches," she warned.

"I told you!" said Ben unhelpfully.

Their luck ran out, as she feared it would. The single, linear path came to a T intersection, splitting off in two directions.

"Which way?" said Bobbie.

"How should I know?" said Ben. "Which direction does your brother like more: right or left?"

"That's not a thing," said Bobbie, and then she shouted, "Johnny! Johnny, where are you?"

Silence followed her question. Silence . . . and then a low, trembling growl. The echo made it difficult to know which way it had come from.

"This way," said Ben, and he turned to the right. "I heard him. I see him!" Ben approached a shambling figure in the dim light. It had its back turned to them as it shuffled aimlessly up the tunnel.

"Ben, stop!" Bobbie shouted. "That isn't Johnny!"

Ben reeled back as the figure turned to face him. It was a zombie, but it was *not* the zombie he was looking for.

Bobbie hurried past him, and with a swing of her sword, she knocked the ghoul momentarily back. But it had its focus on her now, and it kept coming.

Ben came at it from behind, slashing it with his sword and regaining its attention. Bobbie stepped back and watched as he timed his swings expertly, avoiding the zombie's lunges as he hacked away at it. After only a few hits, the zombie crumbled to dust.

"That looked nothing like Johnny," she said.

"Are you kidding me?" said Ben. "You can tell zombies apart now?"

"That thing was almost twice as tall as my brother!" she said. "And he didn't have a lead. And his nose was totally different. Should I go on?"

"Please do," said Ben. "But can you lecture me while we run?"

They continued along their current path, but soon came to a

dead end in the form of an uneven wall of dirt. "Slimeballs," said Bobbie, and Ben tutted.

"I think I'm a bad influence on you," he said. "Come on, this way. Don't worry—we'll find him."

They turned around, retracing their steps to the T intersection and taking the other path.

"I only have three torches left," warned Bobbie. "And I left behind nearly all the coal we found."

Ben cursed under his breath. "Okay. I'm going to backtrack and grab some of the torches off the wall, back the way we came from."

"We can't turn back yet!" said Bobbie.

"We're not. I promise," he said. "But we *need* light down here. I'm just going to retrace our steps for one minute."

"But—"

"The longer we argue, the farther away he gets," he said over his shoulder, already retreating. "Stay there! I'll be back before you know it."

Ben turned the corner, and Bobbie was suddenly alone. The silence, the darkness, the stone above her head, and the worry in her heart—it all pressed in on her. She tried not to peer into the darkness ahead of her and wonder what might be just beyond her vision.

Well, *Johnny*, for one. He was ahead of her somewhere.

She took a step forward. She still had three torches, after all. She could make some progress while she waited for Ben to return.

She waited as long as she could before placing the next torch— toeing the very edge of darkness, determined to make the most of her suddenly limited resource. She should have been spacing them out farther all along, but she never would have thought she'd run out of them so quickly.

Funny how easy it was to take what you had for granted.

As she edged forward, she heard a strange sound ahead. It was a sort of *clack*ing, like dry rocks in a sack, knocking into one another.

And then something flew toward her. If she hadn't been peering forward, she would never have seen it in time. As it was, she just barely had time to dodge it.

She turned around to see what it was. An arrow stuck in the rock wall just behind her.

Something had *shot* at her.

She whirled back around and saw a skeleton emerging from the darkness.

This time, she had her sword ready. She had watched Ben fight the zombie, timing his attacks perfectly so that he hit the zombie each time it lunged within reach. She had used a similar technique against the creeper, and she could do the same thing against the skeleton.

Except the skeleton wasn't coming any closer. It took aim with its bow and fired. This time, Bobbie didn't dodge quickly enough, and the arrow sliced across her arm.

It hurt.

"Get over here and fight me!" she bellowed, brandishing her sword.

It took aim, another arrow already notched in its bow.

Bobbie realized she needed a different strategy. If the skeleton wouldn't come to her, well . . .

Bobbie ran forward, sword raised, and she screamed a ragged war cry.

The skeleton fired its arrow, injuring her again, but she didn't let it stop her. A second later, she was upon the skeleton, striking it again and again in a wild flurry of furious blows. It shattered to pieces, leaving behind only a single intact bone and two arrows.

Bobbie turned at the sound of footsteps and saw Ben approaching her from behind. "Ben!" she said. "I just beat my first skeleton."

Ben's eyes went wide, and he broke out into a run, heading right for her. "You missed one!" he said.

"What?"

Before Bobbie could process his words, Ben had tackled her, dragging her down to the stony ground. She was ready to complain—but then an arrow whizzed by overhead.

"Oh," she said, and turning toward the dark end of the tunnel, she saw another skeleton, bow raised and ready. It was joined by a second, and a third.

"That's a lot of skeletons," she said bleakly. "What should we do?"

"Try not to die," Ben answered, and he surged forward down the tunnel, sword flashing as he closed the distance to the nearest mob. Bobbie followed his example, reasoning that it was better to be in striking range than to hang back and draw fire.

As she advanced, she saw a strange object just past the skeletons. It looked like a small metal cage. A tiny flame burned within it.

"I'll handle the skeletons," Ben told her between swings. "You destroy that spawner with your pickaxe!"

"Spawner?" echoed Bobbie.

"The cage thing! If we don't destroy it, it's going to keep making more skeletons until we're completely overwhelmed!"

Bobbie didn't like the sound of that. She hurried past the skeletons—their ire was directed entirely at Ben, for the moment—and she brought her pickaxe down on the spawner. It broke after just a few blows.

She intended to whirl back around then to run to Ben's aid. But she saw another figure up ahead—one she thought she recognized. Once she placed a torch down, casting a sphere of light that pushed back at the darkness, she was certain.

"Johnny!" she cried.

Her brother had wandered up to the very edge of a rushing subterranean river. At the sound of her voice—did he recognize his name?—Johnny turned to look at her.

But he turned too quickly.

He lost his footing.

Bobbie watched in horror as her brother fell into the raging river and was immediately swept away in its current.

But she only watched for a second. And then she ran forward as fast as she could and dove headfirst into the water.

CHAPTER 24

Bobbie fought to keep her head above water.

It was a losing battle. The current was so strong, and the river took a tortuous path through the pitch-dark underground. How could Bobbie hope to find the surface when she couldn't even tell which way was up?

And how could she find Johnny in all this chaos?

After a little time, even as the river continued to rage, the darkness began to lighten. An eerie orange glow filled the cavern.

She only hoped it wasn't daylight. There would be no protecting her brother from *that*.

And then, suddenly, just as Bobbie was beginning to wonder whether she'd be swept out to sea, the current calmed and the narrow river widened into a tranquil underground lake.

In the eerie orange light, Bobbie was able to see Johnny nearby, struggling to swim. The poor thing was actually trying to *bite* the water, as if he could fight it off or infect it, turning it to his side. She grabbed him from behind, careful to avoid his teeth and claws, and dragged him to shore.

Gripping his lead, Bobbie collapsed onto the dry stone, and Johnny did the same. "Bad baby," she said, breathless, although part of her took some comfort in knowing that Johnny still had a tendency to wander off. It was another reminder that the Johnny she knew was still in there, somewhere.

Bobbie remained splayed out on the ground, allowing herself a moment to catch her breath. As she lay there, a voice rose over the sound of the water.

"Ow!" it said. "Slimeballs!"

Bobbie popped up from her prone position to see Ben swimming in their direction. Bobbie extended a hand, and he took it as he clambered onto shore.

"That was awful," he said, wheezing for breath.

"You followed us!" said Bobbie.

"Well, sure," said Ben. "I've done more idiotic things for less of a payday." He plopped down on the ground. "Not *much* more idiotic, though."

"Right," said Bobbie. She kept forgetting why Ben was *really* there.

She gazed back at the river, and she saw, now, the source of the cavern's strange orange glow. It was lava—a whole cistern of it, roiling and bubbling mere steps away. The sight took her breath away.

Ben lifted his head to follow her gaze. "You look like you've never seen lava before."

"I haven't," she said. "Only in books. It's beautiful."

"From a distance, I guess. But don't touch it," said Ben, and then he turned to Johnny. "That goes double for you, you nocturnal numbskull."

Johnny opened his mouth to growl, and a mouthful of river water poured out.

"That black wall," Bobbie said. "The one that's separating the water from the lava. Is that obsidian?"

"Yeah. Useful stuff, because it blocks lava and explosions," answered Ben. "It forms sometimes where water and lava come into contact. I'd say we should mine it, but our paltry iron pickaxes won't do the job." He pulled himself to his feet. "It can also be a little tricky, mining so close to lava. I once set my boots on fire and had to jump in a lake."

Bobbie, who'd been creeping closer to the edge, took a big step back.

Ben chuckled. "The good news is that the light will keep new monsters from spawning, no torches required." He rolled his shoulders. "We should rest. Maybe eat something. I don't know about you, but I took a couple of arrows back there."

While Bobbie started a campfire with her last piece of coal, Ben set out their beds, and then he ringed them with cobblestone. It only took a few minutes before they had an open-roofed structure with simple openings to serve as a door and windows.

Bobbie blinked furiously at the sight. "You . . . you just built a whole *house* in the time it took me to shake the water out of my boot-gloves."

"Well, sure, but it's pretty basic," Ben said, as if it really were no big deal. "And I had all that stone in my inventory, so why not?"

"You sure would have been handy around Plaintown," Bobbie said. "It was all I could do to keep our fences in shape."

"Speaking of fences," Ben said, and he planted a wooden post in the ground outside the structure.

"Is that for Johnny? Forget it," she said. "I'm not letting him out of my sight again. We can put his post *inside*, please."

"But . . ." Ben looked back at the structure, and he sighed. "Fine. But I'll have to take down a wall and make the place bigger. I don't want the Infant Insidious lurking over my bed while I'm asleep."

After another minute, Ben was satisfied that the interior was large enough to share with Johnny. Bobbie tied his lead to the post, which was in one corner of the structure, while Ben pulled out some food he'd been saving for a rainy day. He was getting tired of melon slices.

"By the way, I'm . . . sorry he got away," he said, setting a pork chop over the fire. He turned to look at Bobbie. "I must not have secured the lead well enough. But I promise it was an accident."

"I know," Bobbie said. "I don't blame you. But the whole thing makes me nervous. The longer it takes us to cure him . . . the better the chance something *bad* will happen to Johnny."

"Something bad," echoed Ben. He smirked. "Like, something *worse* than turning into a mindless zombie."

"He isn't mindless," Bobbie said. She turned to look at her brother, and she saw that he was staring blankly at the wall. And drooling a little. "And anyway, *yes*, there are worse things than being a zombie." Her voice got softer. "At least there's a cure for it. There's a lot of bad stuff that can't be fixed."

"Yeah. Fair enough," said Ben. He looked up, over the walls of their little fort. The light from the lava lit up a vast, hollow space overhead. "We'll find some gold tomorrow. I'm sure of it."

They ate in silence after that, illuminated by the glow of the lava and the fading campfire, each thinking about what tomorrow might bring.

Johnny ate his pork chop raw.

CHAPTER 25

en shouldn't have made promises he couldn't keep. "We'll find some gold tomorrow," he had said, and he'd been so *certain*.

But then, Bobbie was certain that her undead brother wasn't going to devour them in their sleep, and that remained to be seen. Ben had awoken to the unsettling grunts and groans of Johnny as he'd strained at his lead. Bobbie insisted he was just bored—zombies apparently didn't sleep—but Ben thought the half-pint hellion looked *hungry*.

They decided to get some distance from the lava before starting the day's mining. They ended up in a dripstone cave, with massive stalactites that dripped with moisture. Ben couldn't shake the feeling that they looked like fangs bearing down on him from above.

After hours of digging, they had little to show for their efforts. A few chunks of raw copper, some iron, and a lot of coal. Not useless by any means—but not what they were looking for.

"I don't understand," said Ben. "I've had some bad luck before, but this is ridiculous."

"I might have something over here," said Bobbie, and she beckoned him to follow her around a stony corner. Johnny, tied to his post, growled but stayed put.

Bobbie had found a chamber of smooth purple. The material glittered beneath the torchlight. "It's an amethyst geode," Ben said. "There should be clusters of gems here." He ran his hands over the flat, featureless purple. "But it's all been harvested already."

"I did find one piece," Bobbie said, and she held out a single shard of the purple gemstone. "It was lying on the floor, in the shadows, like someone had missed it."

"In the shadows?" said Ben.

"Yeah, that's the other thing," Bobbie said. She pointed to a torch. "I didn't put that there. Is that . . . normal?"

It was not normal.

But it certainly explained some things.

"It's the woodland mansion all over again," he said. "Somebody's been through here already. They scoured the place and took all the good stuff." He shook his head. "Probably a group of people working together, to have been so thorough."

"So we're out of luck?" said Bobbie. "All the gold is gone?"

"We *will* find gold," Ben said, despite his resolution to stop making promises. "We just might have to travel a little farther than I'd planned. Can I have that amethyst shard?"

Bobbie handed it over. "Is it worth something?"

"It's useful," Ben answered, turning it around in his hands. "With this and the copper I dug up earlier, we can craft a spyglass." He stashed the shard in his inventory. "I don't like being underground for so long, and our little river ride got me all turned around. I think we should head back to the surface and see where we are." He shrugged. "Maybe we can find a badlands biome. You can find gold aboveground there sometimes, in the mountains."

"I like the sound of that," Bobbie said. "Only . . ."

"What?" asked Ben.

"*You* have to break the news to Johnny," she said, pulling the carved pumpkin from her inventory. "He really hates this thing."

Making their way up to the surface took longer than it had taken to carve a path down. Rather than cut blindly through stone and risk hitting a lava flow, Ben opted to build a staircase. They were deep enough that it took some time. And it took *more* time to coax Johnny up the staircase, one hop after another. Bobbie was practically dragging him at one point, pumpkin helmet and all.

If Ben didn't know better, he'd think the zombie boy was pouting. "Don't be so glum. That pumpkin really suits you!" Ben told him. "It brings out the beady little intensity of your blood-red eyes."

Johnny growled and swiped in Ben's direction, and Ben laughed.

"Please stop taunting him," Bobbie said to Ben. "And you," she said, turning to Johnny. "No hitting. No fussing. The pumpkin is for your own good. We have no idea whether it's day or night up there."

When he finally broke through dirt to feel the sun on his face, Ben experienced a wave of relief. "Ah, sweet sunlight!" he said. "I almost forgot what it felt like."

Bobbie blinked furiously. "Me too," she said. "I feel like I've been holding my breath for days."

"Nothing to fear up here—not while the sun is up," Ben said, hopping up onto the grass and offering her a hand. "No phantoms, no skeletons, no zombies . . . present company excluded," he added, as Johnny clambered up behind Bobbie. "It's an undead-free existence as long as that beautiful yellow square is shining down on us."

"Then let's move quickly," Bobbie said. "Because in my experience, the weather can change in the blink of an eye."

The weather remained bright and clear, however, as the trio continued to climb. Ben knew that they'd have to get some altitude in order to get the lay of the land, and as luck would have it, the Overworld had provided, in the form of a nearby mountain.

A nearby, quite *steep* mountain.

"Up and down and up again," complained Bobbie. "The life of an adventurer is *exhausting*."

"Imagine how your brother feels," said Ben. "He's the first zombie who's ever had a list of rules to follow."

"And he's doing so well," said Bobbie, and she patted him on his round orange helm.

At last, they reached the peak of the mountain. Ben got right to work, setting down a crafting table, pulling his materials together, and—

Getting hit in the face with a snowball.

"Bleh?!" he said.

Bobbie's laugh tinkled on the icy air. "Ben! It's snow! *Snow!*"

"I can see that," said Ben, wiping the snow off his face. "And I can also taste it. What's the big idea?" Then, as he watched her hopping and prancing and rolling around like a deranged pig, he realized something. "You've never seen snow before!" he said.

"Nope!" said Bobbie, and she laughed. "It's sort of amazing. Better than lava, anyway!"

"It's all right," Ben said, but he smiled despite himself. He'd seen plenty of snow and tended to think of it as an obstacle, if he thought of it at all. But seeing Bobbie prancing around, it was hard not to imagine it through her eyes. It *was* sort of magical.

Even Johnny, tied to his post, seemed entranced as the snow creaked beneath his feet.

Bobbie lobbed another snowball at him, and he dodged it. "No fair," he said, laughing. "I don't have a shovel!"

"Who said I was interested in a fair fight?" she asked, sticking her tongue out. Her third snowball was aimed, gently, at Johnny, who appeared utterly confused by the entire thing.

Ben got back to business, working the copper and amethyst into a functioning spyglass. With the new tool in hand, he stepped to the edge of the peak and gazed outward. Bobbie, huffing with exertion, trudged through the snow to stand beside him.

She gasped. "The Overworld . . . it's so *big*," she said. "From up here, it looks just like one of Cartographer Haven's maps."

"This is nothing," Ben said as he peered through the spyglass. "I've been exploring for years, and I haven't seen a fraction of the Overworld. It's bigger than I can even wrap my head around."

Ben handed her the spyglass and watched as she spun to look in every direction. "I didn't see any badlands out there," he told her. "But there are some other biomes we might want to check out. I saw a desert, and if there's a pyramid there, we could find some good loot."

"What about that village?" said Bobbie.

"Village? Where?"

"There," she said, pointing, and she handed him the spyglass. "You can just see it through the trees."

"I see it now," said Ben. "Good eye. Only—what is *that*?" Just beyond the village, rising above it, was a featureless gray monolith. Now that he'd noticed it, Ben could see it even without the spyglass. It was that big—and that out of place.

"How do you feel about a little detour?" he asked Bobbie.

"Those people might need help," she said. "So just try to keep me away."

CHAPTER 26

Ben was determined not to get his hopes up. The village in the distance would almost certainly be as devastated as the last two villages he'd found.

Then again, Plaintown had provided an unexpected bounty—Bobbie herself. Maybe this village, too, would have survivors? Maybe they'd find a new ally, even amidst devastation?

But as they drew closer to the village, Ben kept the real mystery at the forefront of his mind. "Do you see it?" he asked. "The gray building, at the back?"

Bobbie peered ahead, past the inviting spruce-and-stone structures, and her eyes found the boxy cobblestone monstrosity looming behind the village proper.

"I see it," she confirmed. "Any closer to figuring out what it is?"

"Your guess is as good as mine." Ben sighed, then pulled out his sword. "But let's be ready for trouble. Again."

A fence ringed the village. That, too, was unusual, although Ben had often wondered why more villages didn't put up some sort of defensive perimeter. It made sense, in a dangerous world, to put barriers between yourself and the monsters.

But Ben noticed there were no gates along the length of the fence. And he had to wonder—was it here to keep unwanted visitors out?

Or was it here to keep something inside from escaping?

Bobbie cut through the fence without hesitating. "Look at you," Ben said. "From fence mender to fence dismantler in a few short days."

"That's me," said Bobbie. "Bobbie, smiter of fences."

But Ben noticed that, as soon as they'd all passed through, Bobbie replaced the broken piece.

He smiled. He didn't actually want her to change. Not too much.

"This is way too familiar," Ben said, approaching the first building. Its door had been blown off its hinges. Bobbie, solemn again, said nothing.

"Yep," Ben said, confirming that the home's chest was empty. "Looks like the same deal as before."

"Wait," Bobbie said. "Something's different this time."

Ben watched her as she turned in a slow circle, taking in the details of the home. She narrowed her eyes, obviously struggling to put her suspicions into words.

Finally, her eyes lit up. "The bed," she said. "There's no bed."

"That's strange," Ben said. "Were any beds missing from the last town?"

"Not that I noticed," said Bobbie.

"Let's check next door," Ben suggested.

It was the same situation in the next house, and the one after that. The entire village appeared empty of villagers, loot . . . and beds.

And as they explored, they drew ever nearer to the stone structure.

"No more putting it off," said Ben. "We need to find out what's inside." He began walking around the perimeter, stopping at the first corner, which gave him a view of two sides of the four-sided building. "I don't see any windows, but there's a door."

Bobbie and Johnny followed close behind as he approached the iron door. He pressed his ear against it.

"Anything?" asked Bobbie.

Ben shook his head. "It's too thick." He eyed the button beside the door. "Should I open it?"

Bobbie tied Johnny to his post. "You behave out here," she said. "We'll be right back." Then, at her signal, Ben pressed the button. Immediately, they could hear voices echoing within the building. It sounded like villagers—and they were in distress.

Spurred on by the sounds, Bobbie hurried past him, and he followed her.

"Careful!" she told him, putting up her arms so that he wouldn't rush ahead.

Ben felt a rush of vertigo as he realized they were standing on a narrow stone platform set above a deep chasm. There were plentiful torches set about the space, providing light in lieu of any windows. But there was also light coming from below; Ben recognized the telltale glow of lava.

A staircase led down from their platform, but for now, they ignored that. Straight ahead, in the center of the space, was something that demanded their immediate attention.

"Zombies," said Ben.

There were two of them, and they soon caught sight of Ben and Bobbie. Groaning and grasping, they stepped forward—but they were stopped by the fence that ringed them, enclosing them upon their own separate platform of stone. The zombies, mindless, didn't seem to realize that they were trapped within a corral and that Ben and Bobbie were forever out of reach.

The only other features within the room were the cells—four of them in total, one in each corner of the structure. Ben could see right inside them, because their walls were made of glass. They were like giant aquariums, but instead of fish, they contained people. Five villagers stood imprisoned in each glass box, each with their own bed and nothing more.

Bobbie gasped. "We have to get them out of there."

"I'm with you," said Ben. "But let's be careful about it." He peered over the edge of their platform, toward the warm glow of lava below.

They briefly considered constructing walkways to the glass cells, but Ben's vertigo threatened to get the best of him. In the end, they decided to come at the problem from another direction, going back outside and then cutting into the cells from the exterior of the building. The harried villagers honked at one another and at Ben and Bobbie, making a great racket in their relief and gratitude.

"One at a time, *please*," said Bobbie. "We're here to help, but we need to understand what happened here."

Ben, realizing he was of no use in communicating with the villagers, slipped away, returning to the inside of the building. Moving slowly, he descended the interior staircase, curious to see where it would lead.

He wasn't surprised to find a small pool of lava below. But he was surprised to see something moving within it. Surprised—and horrified.

It was an iron golem. It was on fire, struggling to keep its head above the lava even as it burned. Ben instinctively reached out to it, but what could he do? Even if he could reach it in time, he'd only doom himself to a fiery death by touching it.

He was too late anyway. As he watched, the light in its eyes went dark. It melted to slag, a smear of silver swirling amidst the incandescent orange.

The stairs descended deeper, and so did Ben. Below the lava, which had been contained within a glass pit, there was a series of hoppers—functioning like funnels, the hoppers had been set up to sort materials that fell into them from above. The hoppers, in turn, fed into a treasure chest. Ben opened the chest, suspecting that he knew what he'd find.

He was right, but the sheer quantity of it staggered him.

Within the chest, he found neat stacks of iron ingots. *Thousands* of iron ingots.

This place had been built with one thing in mind: harvesting golems of their iron. Thousands of ingots meant that hundreds of golems had met a fiery end much like the one Ben had just witnessed.

His heart felt heavy at the thought.

"Ben?" said a voice. He turned to see Bobbie watching from the stairs. "What did you find?"

"Iron. A lot of it," he said. "The villagers must have been making golems constantly. Did you learn anything from them?"

"From what I could understand, there was a zombie attack. They tried to flee, but someone had built a fence around the entire village. They were herded toward this building, and then trapped. They've been kept here for weeks."

"And how did they feel about it?"

Bobbie frowned. "They felt *scared*."

"That's why those zombies were up there with them," said Ben. "With glass walls, the villagers felt constantly threatened by the zombies. And as long as they felt that way, they were willing to make golems." He pointed at the pool of lava, which appeared to float above them in its glass enclosure. "The golems were melted to slag, and the hoppers funneled the remains into the chest."

Bobbie's mouth was a thin line. "This is so *typical*," she said. "It's just like adventurers to exploit villagers. To treat them like they don't matter. I've seen it happen all my life."

Ben almost felt the need to apologize. But he'd never have taken things this far—even if it was sort of brilliant, in a way.

"Do the villagers know who did this?" he asked.

"I think there are at least two of them," Bobbie answered. "They come back to collect the iron every few nights." She paused, then added, "They should be due back tonight, in fact."

"That's good news. Because I'd really like to meet them. But first . . ." He opened the chest and grabbed a handful of ingots. "I think we're overdue for some new gear, don't you?"

CHAPTER 27

en tried hard not to think about where his new armor had come from. He was still haunted by the sight of the iron golem as it melted right before his eyes.

But there was no bringing the golem back. And putting the iron to use themselves meant depriving the iron farm's masterminds of their spoils.

Although, once he heard them speak, Ben immediately decided that "mastermind" was far too generous.

It was night, and Ben and Bobbie had perched atop the roof of the nearest house. From their vantage point, they had a good view of the iron factory, but would themselves be difficult to spot. They secured Johnny in one of the houses a bit farther down the path, where his growls wouldn't draw attention. The villagers they'd hidden behind a newly constructed wall in the village temple. If anyone went looking for them, they'd come up empty—unless that person had a comprehensive knowledge of the temple's blueprint.

And the pair who came around to collect the day's iron did not strike Ben as the type to have comprehensive knowledge of anything.

"Dude," said one of them, seeing the multiple holes in their factory. "What happened?"

"Doesn't look good," said the other. "Check inside."

"*You* check inside," was the response.

At length, one of them at last went inside. Ben crept to the edge of the roof to get a better look at the one who'd stayed behind. It was a girl, and she looked tough, with muscular arms and cold eyes. She held a diamond axe at her side.

As Ben and Bobbie watched, the second one emerged from the factory. He was wiry, with an edgy, thrumming sort of energy, like a taut string. He wielded a crossbow and a frown. "It's no good, Hatchet," he said, bouncing from foot to foot. "We been robbed."

"What do you mean? The iron, too?"

"Yeah," he said. "Villagers're gone. Iron's gone—just an empty chest down there." He shrugged. "Zombies are still there."

"Well, that's something, at least," said Hatchet. "I'd hate to tell the boss we lost any of his pets."

Ben and Bobbie exchanged a look. On the one hand, the idea that these two had a boss made some sense. They definitely gave off "hired muscle" vibes.

But zombies as . . . pets? Who would think that was a good idea?

"Let's load them up," said Hatchet. "Then check the traps on the way back."

Bobbie gave Ben a questioning look, but he could only shrug. He waited for the two strangers to disappear into the factory, then he leaned over to whisper, "I want to follow them . . . but let's keep our distance." Bobbie nodded.

Soon, the two figures reappeared. This time, they were pursued by the pair of zombies. With practiced speed, they stayed out of reach of the zombies, but close enough to draw the mobs forward. "Get the trapdoor, Flip," said Hatchet, and the wiry one darted ahead to open a hinged door that had been set into the ground. Hatchet led the zombies to the edge of it, then punched them, knocking them into the opening.

Flip giggled. "Nice," he said.

"Safer than using my axe," said Hatchet. "Don't want to do any permanent damage, right?"

"I still think we could spare one or two," Flip said, and he jumped into the hole. Hatchet followed immediately after, shutting the trapdoor behind her.

Bobbie exhaled. Ben knew how she felt; he'd almost been afraid to breathe. The trapdoor had brought the mercenaries perilously close to their hiding spot.

Ben waited a few moments before he slid off the roof and padded over to the trapdoor. Now that he'd seen it in action, he wondered how he'd missed it before. Echoing his thoughts, Bobbie whispered, "We must have walked right over that thing."

Ben pressed his ear to it. He agonized over how long to wait. He did not want to run afoul of those two. But if he waited too long, they'd get away. Unless they were immensely careless, they'd be impossible to track once they were underground.

Finally, he couldn't stand to wait any longer. He opened the door.

His jaw dropped at what he saw.

Just belowground, there was a cobblestone tunnel.

With torches placed at regular intervals.

And a rail.

"Um," said Ben. "That looks . . . *very* familiar."

He looked up, his eyes meeting Bobbie's . . . and he saw her gaze harden as she put the pieces together.

"Ben, tell me if I'm wrong," she said. "But I'm beginning to think . . . maybe the siege that destroyed my village . . ."

"It wasn't an accident," said Ben.

CHAPTER 28

They decided to follow the rail.

Compared to digging their way through the underground, it was easy. All the work had been done for them. They only had to retrieve Johnny from his hiding place, hop through the hatch, and walk.

It bothered Bobbie that they weren't sure they were going in the right direction. They stopped periodically to listen, straining their ears and peering into the dark, but they neither heard nor saw any sign of Flip and Hatchet or their undead captives.

But Ben had consulted his map, which showed the way back to Plaintown. And they had decided to walk in the other direction, away from Bobbie's home. Otherwise it felt too much like they were retracing their steps.

"We should have checked beneath Savannaton," Bobbie said. "I bet this rail extends all the way there, too."

"And maybe even to the woodland mansion," said Ben. "These people are *thorough*."

As they walked, Bobbie lost track of time completely. With unchanging scenery and no sun and no moon to go by, time became vague and elastic. She got hungry every so often, and they would stop to eat. Sometimes Johnny would utter a rattling growl from behind her. Otherwise, one moment bled seamlessly and endlessly into the next.

Bobbie began rummaging through her inventory. She pulled out the strange idol they'd taken from the evoker. She waved it over Johnny's head. Poked him with it. Nothing happened, except that Johnny became aggravated and swiped at the thing.

She put the idol away and took out her nautilus shell. She ran her hands over its smooth surface, letting the swirls of the shell draw her in. The effect was almost hypnotic.

With a jolt, Bobbie realized that something was missing from her inventory. The emeralds—she'd left them behind when they'd been digging for gold. She'd put them in a chest and never gone back for them!

Her heart sank at the realization. It was hopeless to think they could find their way back to that area, especially after the river had gotten them so turned around. But Ben was counting on those emeralds. The promised payment was the only reason he'd agreed to help Bobbie in the first place.

They'd grown closer on their quest. Ben even seemed to like Johnny a little bit, sometimes. But would he stick around if he knew he wouldn't get paid? Would he still want to help them, or would Bobbie be left to fend for herself?

She decided she couldn't take the risk. She didn't dare tell him the truth.

"What is it?" Ben asked, and only then did Bobbie realize she'd stopped walking.

"Oh, uh," she said. "It's just . . . this shell. It's so pretty."

"Can I see it for a second?" he asked.

"Sure," she said, and she handed it to him. "But be careful with it. I know you don't think it was worth the expense, but—"

"Shush," he said. "Listen." And he put the shell up to her ear.

A faint sound rose from the shell. It sounded almost like Ben's "shush," but softer, and it rose and fell in an endless cycle. Bobbie found it calming.

"What is that?" Bobbie asked.

Ben shrugged, bringing the shell to his own ear. "People say it's the sound of an ocean, trapped inside the shell by a powerful witch." He returned the shell to her and resumed walking. "I don't think that's true. But oceans are eerily quiet, so maybe."

"You've seen one? An ocean?" As she fell into step beside him, Bobbie took care to stow the shell away safely—it felt even more precious to her now. "I was hoping to catch a glimpse of one through the spyglass, when we were up on the mountain. I've only ever seen one on maps, though, and it looked so . . . so big and so *blue*. Like the sky came down to the ground and settled in for a nap." She turned to Ben. "But you've *seen* one. What was it like?"

"Well . . . big," said Ben. "And blue. You've got the right idea, really."

Bobbie rolled her eyes. "You've got to do better than that. We've been walking down this tunnel for what seems like years and I'm starting to wonder if *I'm* a zombie."

"Okay, okay," said Ben. "The truth is, yeah, an ocean is impressive when you see it at a distance. They're as vast as anything. The scale of them . . . !" He shook his head. "But at the same time, that's missing the point entirely."

Bobbie didn't understand. "What do you mean?"

"An ocean isn't the featureless blue plane you see on a map.

That's just the *surface*. The real magic is underneath." He smiled. "There are fish in colors you could barely imagine. And the coral is even more colorful! There are dolphins, and squids, and guardians that shoot laser beams—I'm slightly less fond of those guys, but they do look cool . . ." He laughed. "This one time, I heard rumors about an island, somewhere out on the water—an island where everything was made out of mushrooms. The trees were giant mushrooms. The ground was some kind of squishy fungus. Even the cows were made of mushrooms!"

"How does *that* work?" Bobbie asked, skeptical.

"I don't know!" said Ben. "Logan and I decided we had to see it for ourselves. We built a couple of rowboats and went out searching for the island. We ended up befriending this dolphin—we named it Squeaklebeak—and Squeaklebeak showed us the way to a *shipwreck*. We never found the mushroom island, if it even exists . . . but that was a really great adventure."

"I knew it," said Bobbie. "The ocean sounds amazing."

"It *is* amazing. The whole world is amazing, really, once you peek beneath the surface." He shook his head. "I guess that's what the maps can't show you."

"I guess so," said Bobbie.

"All right," Ben said, shoving her shoulder lightly with his own. "It's your turn. Regale me with an adventure."

"Me?" Bobbie scoffed. "I don't have any stories."

"Oh, come on. There was that one about the chicken and the fox."

"It was a rabbit."

"Right! The fox and the rabbit. That was a great story."

Bobbie sighed. "I never . . . never went anywhere. Never did anything."

Behind them, Johnny groaned mournfully.

Ben laughed. "I think *he* thinks you're being too hard on your-self."

"Yeah," said Bobbie, and then, more firmly, "*Yeah*. I never traveled—only far enough to get lumber or sugar cane. But I was a part of a community." She turned to Ben. "Most people in my village had a job—one specific thing they were good at, and they'd do that thing every day. But I did a little bit of everything." She smiled. "I helped whoever needed help. Learned enough about every job so that I could be of use to anyone. And I made sure the village never ran low on supplies." Johnny gurgled. "*And* I still found time to play with Johnny. Which usually meant trying to find where he had wandered off to."

"I'm jealous," said Ben.

"Ha!" said Bobbie. "Yeah, right. The big-time adventurer, jeal-ous of the part-time babysitter? Tell me another one."

"No, I'm serious," said Ben. "I never had roots. Never had any-thing to go *back* to after an adventure." His eyes fell to the ground. "I think that's why I was so happy when Logan took me under his wing. He told me I had a lot to learn, and he was willing to teach me. He didn't ask for anything in return—just first dibs on any resources I found."

Bobbie frowned. "I mean, that's not nothing . . ."

"We had bases, sometimes, when there was an area that we wanted to explore in depth. One time, we even set up a temporary headquarters in an abandoned temple we found." Ben's eyes lit up at the memory, but only for a moment. "We never stayed in one place for long, though. I never really had a home."

"Total freedom," said Bobbie. "I guess I can see how it would leave a person unmoored."

"But stay in one place your whole life, and you miss out on a lot," Ben put in. "Maybe the answer is somewhere between the extremes."

Bobbie thought on that as silence settled over them and they continued their endless march. She'd been so focused on curing her brother that she hadn't given any thought to what would come afterward. She had assumed they would return home—to their house, their village.

But was it still home?

What was a home without any people in it?

She was so caught up in her thoughts that she didn't notice the strange sound at their backs.

"Listen," whispered Ben, and he came to a dead stop. "Do you hear that?"

Bobbie stopped, and now she *did* hear it. A rushing sound, and the creak of old wheels.

And then, a voice, shouting: "Make way! Clear the tracks!"

Bobbie reacted with only seconds to spare. She leaped back, pulling Johnny away from the rail; Ben did the same, moving in the opposite direction. A pair of minecarts sped between them, moving so fast that Bobbie had time to gather only a few impressions.

There was a person in the first minecart, a boy in a leather helm.

He looked vaguely apologetic and a little queasy.

Following in his wake, a second minecart contained . . . Bobbie thought they were *eggs* of some kind, but they didn't look like chicken eggs.

Johnny grumbled with complaint at the sudden jostling. "Sorry, buddy," she said. "But we almost got run over by . . . what *was* that?"

Ben shook his head, his eyes wide with bewilderment. "Were those turtle eggs?" he asked.

Johnny growled again, and he pulled on his lead, hard. "Johnny, calm down," Bobbie said. "It's fine."

"What's got into him?" asked Ben. "He seems really agitated."

"Yeah," said Bobbie. "I thought he was mad at me, but . . . it's like he's trying to get my attention . . ."

A growl rose in Johnny's throat, and it seemed to reverberate all along the tunnel, building upon itself, until Bobbie felt she might be bowled over by the unearthly wail that passed over her.

Ben shuddered. "Creepy," he said, but then he smiled mischievously. "I want to try." He cupped his hands around his mouth, planted his feet, and cried, "Echo!"

Another immense, animalistic growl reverberated from down the tunnel.

Ben's eyes went wide. "That wasn't an echo."

"Ben," said Bobbie, "I think something else is coming this way." She heard shuffling footfalls, rasping grunts, and plaintive groans. "A *lot* of something else," she said.

She knew what was coming their way—knew it in her gut. But she was still surprised by the scale of it.

A wave of zombies stepped into the torchlight. A *stampede*. The far end of the tunnel was choked with the undead.

The zombies had seen them. Their legs churned faster. Their arms opened to receive them. Their mouths yawned open, slavering with hunger.

Bobbie wanted to run, but she stood rooted to the spot.

There was nowhere to run. Nowhere to hide.

This time, there would be no escape from the zombie horde.

CHAPTER 29

"**F**ight or flight?" asked Ben.

"Wh—what?" asked Bobbie. Ben could see that she was reeling from the sight of the horde as it bore down on them.

"Do we fight them?" he asked, and he turned his new iron sword so it gleamed in the torchlight. "Or do we try to run?"

"We can't fight them," said Bobbie.

But Johnny had other ideas.

As Ben watched, Bobbie's brother tugged against her grip. The lead slipped right through her grasp, and though Ben leaped for it as it snaked across the ground, the boy zombie was too fast. He was loose—and lunging toward the horde.

Johnny waded into the throng of zombies, slashing at several of the mobs before climbing on top of one. From his perch atop the zombie's shoulders, Johnny had a perfect opportunity to bash his foe over and over again, while the beleaguered zombie tried and failed to reach Johnny with its teeth.

"He's doing a good job, actually," said Ben.

"He's outnumbered twenty to one!" said Bobbie, and she drew her sword. Whatever hesitation she'd felt before, it had evaporated in the face of Johnny's peril. She flung herself forward, slashing out at the nearest zombie, clearly intent on hacking her way to Johnny's side.

"For the record, my vote was going to be for *flight*," said Ben. "Not that anybody asked me!"

With a long-suffering sigh, Ben joined the fray. He sidled up beside Bobbie but stayed on her left, giving her plenty of room to maneuver with her sword—there was a rhythm to fighting zombies, and she seemed to have gotten the hang of it.

The narrowness of the tunnel worked to their advantage. While the full horde pressed forward, no more than five zombies could reach them—as long as they held the line.

But even five zombies outnumbered them.

Their troubles began in a moment of triumph. Bobbie felled one of the ghouls, reducing it to a scrap of rotten flesh. Ben felt a momentary thrill of victory—maybe they had this, after all? But the fallen zombie left an opening, and as another zombie rushed forward to fill it, it was able to slip past Bobbie's defenses.

Seeing Bobbie take a hit threw Ben off, and he was on the receiving end of the horde's next successful hit. Their rhythm faltered, and the horde began to slip past them. Once they were surrounded, there would be no hope of winning.

So Ben did something desperate.

"What are you doing?" Bobbie asked, noticing that he'd put his sword away. "Ben! I can't defend us all."

"Just a few seconds," Ben said, and as his new armor soaked up the brunt of the horde's attacks, he was glad they'd taken that iron. Without it, he would have fallen by now.

Even *with* it, this was risky.

With his hands free, Ben was able to pull the carved pumpkin from his inventory. Straining across the biting, rending horde, he plunged the helmet over Johnny's head.

Johnny howled in protest, but the pumpkin stayed on him as he bucked. Falling from the shoulders on which he was perched, he was newly vulnerable, and several zombies turned to attack him while he was prone.

Bobbie screamed. "What were you thinking?" she asked him, swinging her sword for all she was worth. Two more zombies fell to her attacks.

Ben didn't have time or breath to explain himself. Every second counted now. He pulled a pickaxe from his inventory and, leaping up, he began to cut away at the dirt ceiling overhead.

Within seconds, sunlight poured into the tunnel. Ben blinked, momentarily blinded, but he didn't let that stop him. He kept swinging his pickaxe, knocking more dirt away, cutting a line of light across the dark.

The stench was almost overpowering as dozens of zombies caught fire simultaneously.

"Grab him!" Ben directed, and as he pulled Bobbie clear of the fracas, she pulled Johnny backward by his lead. Even with the comically large helmet, the zombie boy's bewilderment was obvious. He didn't resist Bobbie's tugging, seemingly transfixed by the sudden light show, and she was able to attach his lead to a post without any problems.

The zombies kept coming, but they had lost any real sense of menace. As those in the front fell, engulfed in flame, others advanced at a staggered pace, impeded by their fallen horde-mates and catching fire as they entered the patch of sunlight.

With Johnny tied to his post, Ben and Bobbie were easily able to find their rhythm again, knocking back any ghoul who made it into their melee range. It was only a matter of stalling for time until the fire had done its work.

As the last zombie crumbled to dark ash before them, Ben's knees gave out. Physically, he was fine—he could already feel his body healing itself—but whatever reserves of courage and will-power he'd drawn upon gave out once the danger was gone. It struck him all at once how close they'd all come to dying.

Bobbie, by contrast, seemed totally energized by the entire ordeal. "Ben, that was amazing," she said, and she pumped her sword in the air. "You saved Johnny!"

"It was . . . it was nothing," Ben said, wheezing.

"How did you know it was daytime?" she asked. "I'd totally lost track."

"Yeah, about that," said Ben. "Lucky guess."

That took some of the wind out of Bobbie's sails. "You mean—you didn't know? But if not for the sunlight . . ." She stared mutely at him, realizing just how close they'd come to disaster.

"Very, *very* lucky guess," said Ben.

CHAPTER 30

After their battle in the tunnel, Bobbie watched as Ben built a wall, cutting right across the railway. He knocked a few of the rails loose for good measure.

"I would feel bad about messing with somebody's build," he explained, "but I'm more certain than ever that these people are up to no good." He paused to survey his work, slapping dirt off his hands. "And this will make it harder for them to sneak up on us again."

Bobbie found it difficult to argue. She only hoped that the boy in the minecart wouldn't send Hatchet and Flip after them from the other direction.

But the tunnel remained empty and quiet as they made their way ever forward. Bobbie found it impossible to remain on high alert for long. It was exhausting to strain her ears for signs of pursuit that might never come.

And her mind kept coming back to Ben. He'd been brave in their fight against the zombies. But she'd come to expect that by now. And, in a way, bravery was easy when you were in an inescapable fight.

But what had struck her was that he'd put his weapon down — he'd made himself vulnerable, had let himself be hurt — because he'd been determined to protect Johnny. The thought that Johnny might be collateral damage in their fight had been unacceptable to Ben.

Bobbie hadn't realized how alone she'd felt until she suddenly realized she had a true ally in Ben.

"You were brave back there," she told him.

Ben puffed out his chest. "I was, wasn't I?"

Aaaand that ruined it. Why couldn't he just take a compliment without letting it go straight to his head?

Bobbie had to keep his ego in check somehow. For both their sakes.

"Good thing it wasn't spiders," she said. "You're weirdly useless around spiders. What's that about?"

Ben deflated. "Why does it have to be *about* something? Spiders are scary."

"I don't know," said Bobbie. "I mean, they aren't *cute*. But they're really just animals. Although . . ." She grinned. "I guess you're afraid of llamas, too."

Ben scoffed. "I am not afraid of llamas," he said. "I don't like getting spat on. That's a very common and reasonable personality trait!"

"Yeah, okay," said Bobbie. "But that's sort of my point. You have a *rational* aversion to llamas. You can explain it with logic." She rubbed her chin. "Zombies are scary because they're relentless. Endermen are scary because they're unpredictable. What makes a spider scary to you?"

"Fear isn't rational, though," Ben argued. "It's the opposite. If anything, we should be afraid of pigs."

Bobbie laughed. "Pigs? What's so scary about pigs?"

"Well, it's not so much pigs themselves. They're harmless enough, right? But do you know what happens when a pig is struck by lightning?"

Bobbie thought about it. "Pork chops?" she guessed.

"Not pork chops." Ben smiled darkly. "Remind me to tell you all about it the next time we set up camp."

It was a short time later when they saw the end of the tunnel.

"Let's be careful. And quiet," Ben whispered.

Bobbie nodded in agreement. Johnny growled.

"Maybe we can tie him up back here?" Ben suggested.

With Johnny secured to a post, Ben and Bobbie crept forward. They could see that the tunnel ended ahead, but the light beyond was dim, so they couldn't tell what it led to.

The rail ended first. There was a minecart in position, ready to be sent down the tunnel with the flip of a switch. "See that lever that looks like a dead torch?" Ben pointed. "That's a *redstone* torch," he whispered. "That means this whole rail system is *powered*. Whoever did this knows their stuff. They might have a whole mining operation going."

Suddenly, sounds rang out from the space beyond the tunnel's exit. It started as a single mournful groan, but then it grew into a nightmarish cacophony. Even Johnny appeared agitated.

"What was *that*?" Bobbie hissed. "Not another zombie horde?"

"No," Ben whispered, and he crept forward to peer into the chamber beyond the tunnel. "I think 'horde' is underselling it."

The tunnel opened out onto a vast, cavernous space—not a cave; there was nothing natural about this space. Its angles were too perfect, its lines too straight. It looked to Ben as if someone had carved a perfect cube out of the subterranean rock . . . and then had filled that cube with zombies.

Hundreds of zombies. More than he could comfortably count. More than he was comfortable *looking* at.

He inched back, away from the opening.

"I've never seen anything like that before," he whispered.

"Good," said Bobbie. "I'd hate to get the impression that was *normal*." She shuddered. "Is it possible it's just an accident?" she asked. "A spawner that's gone out of control, maybe?"

Ben shook his head. "See the space? It looks constructed." He pointed. "There are two more tunnel entrances like this one, and I'll bet those lead to rail tunnels, too. And up above—someone's built a little balcony, so they can keep an eye on the mobs down below."

"So someone built this," Bobbie said. "And they . . . *want* it to be full of zombies. But why?"

"I'd like to learn that myself," said Ben. "But we're not going *that* way. Come on." He hefted his pickaxe. "Let's go upstairs."

CHAPTER 31

I t was night on the surface, and cloudy. With visibility low, it took them a moment to get their bearings. Ben turned in a slow circle to get a sense of their surroundings . . . and he gasped.

A mountain loomed ahead of them. Carved into the side of that mountain was a massive fortress.

"Look at that," he said.

"Oh, I'm looking," said Bobbie. "You realize it's built right over the zombie pit? Or maybe it's more of a zombie dungeon, if it's in the basement of a castle. Oh!" She smiled. "Do you think whoever lives there is locking them up to keep people safe? Maybe they're determined to protect nearby villages, like a feudal lord."

"I love the optimism," said Ben. "But something about the ominous stone edifice looming high above us feels a little *menacing* to me."

Johnny growled, and Ben was going to joke that it was a growl of agreement, but then he realized that Johnny was growling in a specific direction and pulling at his lead.

"What's up with the toothy toddler?" Ben asked.

Bobbie shushed him. "There's somebody over there. I think they're watching us," she whispered.

Ben squinted into the gloom. Bobbie was right—he could just make out a silhouette up ahead. "Hello. We come in peace!" he called, and he held up his empty hands. Casting a sidewise glance at Johnny, who continued to pull on his lead, he muttered, "*Most* of us."

The figure made no reply.

Bobbie tried next. "Do you, um, know anything about who lives there?" She lifted her hand to point at the fortress—and in doing so, she let Johnny's lead slip from her grasp.

Johnny didn't hesitate for a moment. He ran forward, intent on attacking the stranger.

Bobbie called for him to come back, her voice cracking with panic. Ben wasn't sure whether she was more concerned that he'd eat somebody or that he'd get smacked around for trying. Either way, they both ran after him, determined to intercept him before he got within striking distance of the stranger—who remained eerily calm, standing their ground even as a pint-size zombie bore down on them.

Ben saw why as they drew closer. The figure wasn't a person at all. Someone had put a jack o' lantern on top of a hay bale, then affixed wood posts to give the illusion of arms and legs.

"It's a . . . scarecrow?" said Bobbie.

"It's a trap!" said Ben.

His warning came too late. The ground disappeared from beneath their feet, and Ben, Bobbie, and Johnny plunged a short distance into a bare stone room, dimly lit with a single lantern.

A low growl sounded, and Ben said, "You can say that again, Johnny."

"Ben . . ." said Bobbie. "That wasn't Johnny."

Ben scrabbled to his feet just as a creature lunged from the shadows. It was a zombie—a full-grown adult zombie, with grasping hands and open mouth.

Ben was getting well and truly sick of zombies.

And then, before Ben could blink, Johnny leaped forward. Still free of his lead, the young zombie smashed into the older one, shoving it back before it could fall upon Ben.

"All right, brother. Good save!" said Bobbie, and she closed the distance with her sword. She slashed at the hostile mob, stepping back whenever it swiped at her. Johnny tugged at its legs, hampering its movement, and Bobbie was able to destroy it without taking a single hit.

Ben had watched the entire scene without once having to lift his own sword. "You two definitely have the hang of that."

Johnny sniffed at the rotten flesh left behind by the fallen zombie, as if considering its suitability for eating. But he stuck out his tongue and turned away from it in disgust.

"They're not so tough," Bobbie said, "when there's only one of them."

But hundreds of zombies? Ben felt a thrill of dread just remembering what lurked below. "You think this leads down to that dungeon?" he asked, noting a single downward-sloping exit from their hole.

"It must," Bobbie said. "Zombies fall through the trap, and they end up in the pit. I'll bet there are a lot of these traps, all over this area."

"I'll bet you're right," said Ben. He bit his lip. "I should have recognized it for a trap right away. I fell for something similar, back when Logan was training me. Only that trap was way worse than a hole in the ground." He gazed up at the night sky. "We can dig or climb right out of here. But if it had been filled with cobwebs . . ." He shuddered.

"Cobwebs?" Bobbie asked. "What's so bad about cobwebs? We were able to hack our way out of the ones we stepped in, back in Savannaton."

"Webs are like zombies—they're fine one at a time," Ben said. "And when you're on your feet." He leaned against the dirt wall. "But fall into a stack of cobwebs, and they're practically inescapable. *Falling* doesn't feel like the right word, because you're moving so slowly, but you're totally helpless. You're stuck just . . . drifting."

"I don't understand how this was part of your training," Bobbie said.

"Logan wanted to make a point," Ben explained. "I was a noob. Making all kinds of stupid mistakes, and those mistakes put *him* at risk. So he wanted to prove a point." Ben sighed. "He set the trap, and I fell for it. It was this . . . this endless *chasm* of webs in the dark. It felt like I was trapped there forever. And then, the darkness started to recede, and I realized—I was falling right into a pit of lava." Ben shuddered. "Every second I was in the web, I slipped closer to the lava. I couldn't find any way out of it. I couldn't do anything except scream for help, over and over again."

Bobbie put her hands to her mouth. "Ben, that's awful. How cruel!"

Ben shook his head. "Logan was just making a point. He wouldn't have let anything happen to me. He waited until the last minute . . . and then he stepped in and saved me. All it took was a couple blocks of dirt, placed over the lava, and I landed harmlessly on the ground."

"I still think it was cruel," Bobbie said.

"Maybe." Ben shrugged. "But I learned my lesson. It made me a better hero."

"You've made *me* a better hero," said Bobbie. "You've taught me a lot, and you never resorted to scare tactics or power trips to do it. You didn't have to make me feel helpless in order to inspire me." She frowned. "I know it's none of my business," she said, "but this Logan person sounds like a lousy teacher, a terrible friend, and a *rotten* human being."

"I guess I didn't have anything to compare him with," Ben said sadly. "Not on the friend front, anyway."

"You do now," said Bobbie, and she placed a hand on his shoulder.

Johnny tried to bite his other shoulder, but his teeth clacked harmlessly on the iron armor, and Ben assumed the gesture was meant with affection.

Then Bobbie's hand suddenly squeezed. "Ben!" she said. "Do you know what this means?"

"What *what* means?"

"That story you just told me. That's why you're so afraid of spiders!" Her eyes went wide. "You associate spiders with webs, and webs with a traumatic experience that made you feel helpless and scared!"

Ben thought about that. "Yeah, you might have a point," he said. "On the other hand," he added, shuddering, "it could be their beady little eyes."

Bobbie opened her mouth to say something, but she suddenly stopped. Gripping Ben's shoulder more fiercely, she suddenly shoved him back, knocking him prone.

"What was that for?!" he cried. But then he saw the arrow protruding from the wall.

Bobbie had shoved him out of its path just in time.

"I wouldn't move if I was you," said a voice from on high.

Ben didn't move, except to look up. Two figures loomed above, peering over the edge of the trapdoor. One of them was reloading his crossbow; the other brandished a diamond axe and a sneer.

Ben recognized them even in the low light: Flip and Hatchet.

"What are you doing in our trap?" said Hatchet. Her eyes darted to the rotten flesh on the ground. "Did you destroy one of our zombies?"

"The boss isn't gonna like that," said Flip, bouncing on his feet.

"What's your boss want with zombies?" Ben asked.

"Why are you so nosy?" asked Flip, and he took aim.

Ben put up his hands. "Not nosy! Call it . . . professional curiosity."

"Professional?" echoed Hatchet.

"Sure," said Ben. "You say your boss wants zombies?" Ben pulled gently on the lead, and Johnny stepped out from the shadows. "Well . . . we've got a zombie right here."

CHAPTER 32

Whatever Ben was up to, Bobbie hated it.

Hated. It.

Every big sister instinct that she had was ringing with alarm. She didn't like these two heavily armed strangers. She didn't like using Johnny as a bargaining chip to meet their boss. And she didn't like the look of the fortress as they approached. Ben had been right—it was far too imposing to be inviting.

"Are those—*heads*?" Bobbie asked, aghast at the sight of a pair of zombie heads sitting atop posts.

"Welcome to Fort Rot," said Flip.

Hatchet chuckled. "Chop, chop," she said. "Don't fall behind now."

Bobbie turned to Ben. "This is a bad idea," she whispered.

He whispered back, "Don't you trust me?"

Bobbie gave him a long, hard look. "I mean, sure," she answered.

"Wow," Ben said. "You really had to think about that for a minute, didn't you?"

Bobbie scoffed and turned away. "Trust" was an easy word to throw around, but with her brother's safety at stake, she'd be keeping both eyes open.

The fortress was carved from the very mountain. It looked solid and imposing but also very plain. There were no turrets or arched windows, and the entire structure was a dull, monotonous gray. The only exception was a large hanging banner. It was red, and emblazoned upon it was the image of a fearsome black skull above two crossed bones. Ben seemed to recognize it, but he didn't say anything about it. As they ascended the stone staircase, Bobbie saw the wooden portcullis remained closed to them.

"Hey, it's us!" said Flip, and he banged against the gate. "Open up!"

"He better not have wandered off," grumbled Hatchet.

"I'm here!" piped a voice from beyond the portcullis. "One second."

The portcullis lifted, and Hatchet ducked underneath it as soon as it was open. Flip waved Bobbie and the others in ahead of him.

They entered into a sort of courtyard. It was a utilitarian space, boxy and unadorned, with all manner of workstations ringing its perimeter. There was a crafting table, a furnace, an anvil, and more. To Bobbie, it looked like someone had taken an entire village, removed everything of warmth and beauty, and shoved what was left into this single room.

Seeing someone new, Johnny tried to pull away, but Bobbie had a tight grip on his lead. Although outside Johnny's reach, the boy who had been standing at the portcullis controls took a few steps back.

"Uh, this is unusual," said the boy. He was smaller than the other two, younger, with simple leather armor and no visible weapons. "Zombies aren't supposed to come through this way. That's what the tunnels are for."

Hatchet twisted the boy's helmet around, covering his eyes. "We know what the tunnels are for, ya nerd. We dug 'em, didn't we?"

The boy painstakingly realigned his helmet. "Then why . . . ?"

"He's a *special* zombie," Ben said lightly. "Does all sorts of tricks. I'm guessing you're not the boss?"

Flip chortled. "That'll be the day."

"He's on the observation balcony," said the boy. "Should I take them . . . ?"

"We'll take them," said Hatchet. "You take this." And she handed over a small sack of loot. "It's slim pickings out there. I see why the boss wants to move on soon."

Bobbie caught Ben's eye. These *had* to be the people who had been gathering up every available resource. And that meant they *had* to have gold.

But would they part with it? Somehow, she doubted it.

The boy pressed a button, and as the portcullis dropped back into place, he pointed to a nearby chest. "Don't forget—"

"We won't forget," said Hatchet, clearly annoyed. She stomped over to the chest, opened it aggressively, and placed her diamond axe inside it. Flip did the same with his crossbow, then gestured to Bobbie and Ben.

"We'll hold on to ours, if that's okay," said Ben.

Hatchet gave him a dirty look. "That's *not* okay," she said.

"Price of admission to see the boss," said Flip.

Bobbie felt a tingle of anxiety. She didn't like the idea of being defenseless among all these strangers. "Maybe we ought to meet your boss another time," she suggested. "Find neutral territory somewhere."

"Out there?" said Hatchet. "It's *all* Ravager territory. As far as the eye can see."

"And we're the Ravagers," said Flip. "That means you're either our guests . . . or you're trespassers." He glowered at them. "Guests leave their weapons here temporarily. Trespassers have their stuff permanently confiscated."

"Guests it is!" Ben said happily, and he dropped his bow and sword into the open chest.

Bobbie glared at him as she did the same. *Trust me*, he mouthed, and she resisted a sudden urge to stomp on his foot.

"Were those *iron* swords?" Hatchet chortled. "You might as well have held on to them. You'd have a hard time cutting *wheat* with those things."

"Yeah, well," Bobbie said, annoyed, "resources have been hard to come by out there."

"See? What'd I say?" Hatchet said, turning back to the young gatekeeper. "Slim pickings."

Leaving the boy to catalog and organize their loot, Hatchet and Flip led Bobbie and the others up a long, winding staircase. There were basic windows—just empty spaces, really—looking out onto the Overworld, but it was too dark outside for Bobbie to see much. Inside, an abundance of torches illuminated every corner. Johnny grumbled and swiped at more than one burning torch as they passed.

They didn't take the staircase all the way to the top, instead exiting out into a stony hallway lined with doors.

"Are these the living quarters?" asked Bobbie, and she was met with stony silence.

Ben leaned over and whispered, "Nice place, but the tour leaves something to be desired."

A second spiral staircase led down. This one seemed to be an interior space, perhaps going right through the center of the fortress. There were no windows, either in the staircase or the hallway to which it led.

This hallway ended in an open, arched doorway. Their guides—captors?—paused before it.

"I'll wait here and keep an eye on them," said Hatchet. "You fill him in."

Flip scoffed. "*I'll* wait here while *you* fill him in."

A moment of silent tension passed between them. Bobbie half expected them to settle the matter with a fistfight. Was this why they were expected to leave their weapons at the door?

In the end, Bobbie couldn't say what, precisely, had passed between them during their staring contest, only that the impasse was settled. Flip broke eye contact, grumbled "Fine," and stormed through the archway.

Ben winked at Bobbie—she could almost hear him thinking: *Watch this.* He sidled up next to Hatchet and said, "You shouldn't let him push you around like that. Especially in front of, you know, *guests.*"

Hatchet gave him a dirty look. "Mind your own business," she said, and Ben held up his hands in exaggerated surrender.

Throughout all of this, Bobbie kept her brother close, with both hands gripped tight on his lead. He watched the strangers with interest, and she feared that if he slipped her grasp again, he would attack. She wasn't certain, however. His interest might have been mindless hunger, but she thought there was something else in his eyes. Something like the curiosity he used to show around others, before he was transformed.

He *was* still in there somewhere. She was only more convinced as time went on.

Flip returned and gestured for them to enter. Bobbie let Ben go ahead of her, so that she could keep Johnny between them.

She gasped as she crossed out of the hallway and onto the balcony. It didn't overlook the exterior of the castle, as Bobbie had expected. The boy had called it "the observation balcony," after all.

But this balcony overlooked the zombie pit. From this vantage, the sheer number of undead was even more overwhelming to contemplate. She could scarcely see the ground past the crush of shambling green bodies. Anyone who fell into the pit would land right on top of a zombie; anyone who fired an arrow below would be certain to hit one.

That's what "the boss" was doing—firing arrows indiscriminately into the crowd. Bobbie watched as one arrow lodged into a zombie's shoulder. The mob, confused and enraged, lashed out at empty air, unable to understand where the attack had come from.

Bobbie had no love for zombies, but toying with them like this seemed cruel.

She would have expected nothing less from the boy on the balcony, however. She recognized his face as easily as she recognized his cruel laughter.

It was the stranger who had come to Plaintown. The one who had set the Heart Oak aflame.

What was he doing here?

How had he gathered all of these zombies?

And why . . . was he embracing Ben like an old friend?

"Ben!" he cried, drawing the other boy close. "Wow. I never thought I'd see you again."

"Same here," said Ben. "What's new, Logan?"

CHAPTER 33

"**L**ogan?" said Bobbie, and she stepped forward, putting herself between her brother and the other boys. "*This* is Logan?"

The stranger—Logan—grinned. "I'm guessing Ben here hasn't had nice things to say about me. But I'm glad to see him again, and it's nice to meet you."

"So you don't remember me?" she said. "Seriously? You set my village on fire!"

Logan chuckled. "You'll have to be more specific, amirite?" he said, elbowing Ben.

"Heh," Ben said weakly.

Bobbie didn't do it on purpose.

She didn't mean to lose her grip on Johnny's lead.

But as she felt it slipping from her grasp . . . she didn't react as quickly as she could have.

In an instant, Johnny had pushed past her to lunge at Logan. The boy shrieked, jumping back—and, to Bobbie's astonishment, pulling Ben in front of himself like a shield.

Ben put his hands out in an attempt to mollify Johnny. "Hey,

hey buddy," he said. "It's all right." As Johnny approached, Ben eased his hands onto Johnny's shoulders, and Bobbie's brother calmed down. "There, that's it. Logan's a frie—well. Logan isn't for eating."

Ben took up the lead and handed it over to Bobbie. "Drop something?" he asked, and his eyes were accusing.

"Thanks," Bobbie said, accepting the lead and the unvoiced but heavily implied scolding. Ben was right; that had been dangerously irresponsible. If Logan had gone for a weapon instead of retreating . . .

"How did you do that?" asked Logan, and he crept forward.

Johnny growled, and Logan stayed where he was.

"Did you actually *train* a zombie?" he asked, awe in his voice.

"None of your business," said Bobbie, at the same time that Ben said, "We'll tell you all about it."

Ben and Bobbie traded glares.

"We have some questions for *you*, actually," Bobbie said to Logan.

"All right. That's fair." Logan shrugged. "Why don't you two join me for dinner? We'll make a game of it." He grinned. "An answer for an answer. We'll take turns."

The dining hall was an unadorned space, devoid of color and comfort. There were lanterns for light, and furnaces for cooking, and dark windows that likely provided an expansive view of the surrounding landscape during daylight hours—less for aesthetic enjoyment, Bobbie imagined, than for defensive purposes. Everywhere she looked, she was reminded that this was not a home but a fortress.

So who was Logan at war with?

"You almost got me, you know," said Logan. "The old wither rose in the treasure chest trick!" He shook his head and chuckled. "I should have seen it coming."

"Well, you wouldn't have had any trouble if you hadn't *robbed me while I was sleeping*," Ben said, apparently failing to see the humor in any of it.

Logan chuckled again. "Guilty as charged. But be honest. Are you mad that I took off with your stuff? Or are you mad that I did it to you before you could do it to me?"

"The first one!" Ben said hotly. "Why would I even think of doing that to you? We were partners!"

"That was the whole issue," said Logan. "This world's not made for *partners*, Ben. With so much wealth up for grabs . . . well, somebody's got to grab it, eventually. Problem with the steak?"

Bobbie realized belatedly that the question had been directed at her. "Huh?" she said, looking up from the table.

"Your steak. You haven't touched it," said Logan.

"Is that your first question?" Bobbie asked, and he chortled.

"Clever," said Logan. "But no, I don't actually care. Eat the steak or don't. I promise it isn't zombie meat, though, if that's what you're thinking. They're too valuable for that."

Bobbie's eyes flitted up to Johnny, who stood across the room where she could keep him in view. She didn't like the idea that her brother had value to this creep. While it might keep Johnny safer from destruction than he'd otherwise be, it was all too obvious to Bobbie that Logan was a person willing to steal anything of value he could get his hands on.

And he wasn't a very good *boss*, either. When Hatchet and Flip had shown up for dinner, Logan had chased them off, telling them to fend for themselves tonight. Neither of the mercenaries had liked that—Hatchet had glared at Bobbie as if she'd purposely stolen her place—but they hadn't argued, instead skulking off into the fortress interior.

The other boy, the younger one, had been in charge of cooking. He had flitted from one furnace to another, attempting to prepare all three steaks simultaneously. Bobbie had expected he'd then make a fourth meal for himself; instead, he had immediately begun baking their dessert. He stood at a furnace now, keeping well clear of Johnny's range.

"I'll let you two have the first question," Logan said. "Since you're guests and all."

Bobbie knew precisely what she wanted to ask. She opened her mouth to speak—

But Ben blurted out, *"What did you do with all my stuff?"*

Bobbie looked at him, aghast. Was that really what they needed to learn?

Logan crossed his arms. "You know, I had a feeling you'd want it all back. I had my squire gather it up."

"Squire?" said Ben.

"Sure: squire, quartermaster, gatekeeper, cook. Ben does a little bit of everything around here."

At first, Bobbie thought that Logan had gotten their names mixed up. But then the boy at the furnace turned around and waved. "Hi!" he said. "I probably should have introduced myself before. I'm Ben."

Ben gaped like a fish. Finally, he said, *"You're* not Ben. *I'm* Ben."

The boy—Also Ben? Other Ben?—shrunk a little and said, "Sorry."

Bobbie rolled her eyes. "You don't have to apologize to him," she said firmly.

But Ben's—*her* Ben's—focus was entirely on Logan. *"You replaced me with another Ben?!"*

Logan cackled, clearly amused to no end by this. Bobbie couldn't help but think that Ben's emotional reaction was feeding Logan's desire to push buttons.

Logan *liked* to see people squirm, didn't he?

"All right, look," said Logan. "I made a mistake. Is that what you want to hear? I thought I'd be better off alone, but I was wrong. Being alone out there is so much *work*." He leaned back in his chair. "When I came across Hatchet and Flip—fumbling around like a couple of lost, directionless kids—I figured out the solution. Not a partnership, but a *gang*, with a clear hierarchy. We recruited Ben Two a little bit after that. Promised to train him, toughen him up, in exchange for his services."

If "Ben Two" objected to the new nickname, he didn't voice it. He just pointed to a chest across the room and said, "I put all the items you asked for in that chest, sir," then turned back to his furnace.

"Go ahead, Ben One," Logan said. "Your stuff's right over there."

"Ben One" gave Logan a long look, as if suspecting some trick, and when he stood and walked over to the chest, he made a show of checking for traps. Finally content that the chest was safe, he opened the lid and started sorting through the contents.

"My arrows!" he said. "And my pickaxe. And—it's here!" Leaping to his feet, Ben held a gleaming diamond sword up to the sky, striking a pose like an action hero. "Arthropox!" he cried. "Scourge of spiders! Smiter of silverfish!"

Bobbie was anxious, impatient, and generally annoyed, but she still found herself smiling at the sight of Ben's joy. Then her eyes cut to Logan, and she noticed how intently he was watching not just Ben . . . but Johnny, too.

"How'd you train him?" asked Logan. "The zombie boy."

So that's why he'd had Ben's things ready for him. He wanted the chance to observe what would happen when Ben got close to Johnny.

Bobbie had no interest in telling Logan anything, but Ben pressed her. "It's only fair to answer him," Ben said, and he handed her a diamond pickaxe. "I mean, look at that! Quality craftsmanship." He winked. "Keep it. I've got all these cool arrows, too. One that makes you invisible . . . one that lets you breathe underwater . . ."

"Not now, Ben," Bobbie said, and she turned to face Logan. "To answer your question, I 'trained' him by treating him like a human being. You know, with love and respect. And a lot of patience." She frowned. "I sort of doubt you'd be any good at that."

"Ouch," said Logan. "Still sour about that old tree?" He pinned her with his gaze. "Or did something else happen to your precious little village after I left?"

"It's *your* turn to answer a question," said Bobbie.

"Happy to," Logan said lightly. "But let's move this to the roof. You've *got* to see the view." He smiled. "It's positively killer."

CHAPTER 34

They followed Logan. Bobbie tried to listen as he showed them around the grounds, but her mind was racing. She paid attention, however, when Logan showed them his menagerie of turtles. For breeding purposes, he explained.

"I don't know why, but zombies will go out of their way to stomp turtle eggs." Logan chuckled. "So the eggs come in handy when you need to control which way a zombie's gonna go. Helps you herd the horde, you could say."

By this point, Bobbie was nearly vibrating with anger. The more time she spent with Logan, the more her suspicions about him began to seem irrefutable.

If she was right, they were dealing with a monster more terrifying than any zombie.

Logan led them through the building and up another staircase, at last coming to a grand platform that stood atop the fortress and just below the pinnacle of the mountain. A great obsidian throne stood nearby, nestled into the crags, and to the east—

Bobbie gasped at the sight of the sun rising over the ocean.

"Nice view, right?" said Logan, and he clambered atop the oversize blackstone throne. "Fit for a king, I'd say."

"Is that what you're up to here?" asked Ben. "King of the zombies?"

Logan waved his hand dismissively. "The zombies are just a tool. A means to an end. The goal is the same as it always was—loot."

"Speaking of loot," said Ben, "there were a few things missing from that chest. Some emeralds, some gold . . ."

Logan fiddled with a red-tipped scepter that had been built into the wall beside the throne. "I'm rich now. I'm sure I can have Ben Two scrounge up some emeralds for you."

"Make it eight ingots of gold, and we can call it even," said Ben. "And then we'll get out of your hair and let you get back to counting your riches."

"Hold on," said Logan. "You haven't heard my pitch yet."

"Enough!" said Bobbie. "I'm sick of playing games, of—of *humoring* you." She hefted the diamond pickaxe Ben had given her, wielding it like a weapon. Ben stepped in front of her, tried to calm her down, but she ignored him, keeping her eyes on Logan in his ostentatious throne. "Logan. Did you have something to do with what happened to Plaintown?"

Logan held up his hands. "Guilty as charged," he said glibly. "Plaintown was our trial run."

"What does *that* mean?" Bobbie snarled. Sensing her distress, Johnny snarled, too.

When Logan answered, he addressed Ben instead of her. "You remember what it was like, Benny? Long hours spent in the dark, digging at random for loot. Then happening on a village by chance, and hoping they'd have something worth trading for—or taking." Logan swept his arms out. "What we needed was a *system*. A way to be organized about our plundering."

"It was never about the plundering for me," Ben argued.

"Right. Sure," Logan said. "You can fool yourself and your little friend here, Ben, but you can't fool me. I know you like a payday as much as I do." His visage darkened. "And I figured out the ultimate payday, Ben. I found a way to convert villages into a sort of farm for iron—to make them work *for* me, instead of just taking up space. It's actually sort of ingenious." He grinned. "I've got this army of zombies, right? I send them into a village—using tunnels, so they sneak right past the defenses. The zombies cause a panic, and then the Ravagers step in and do what we do."

Bobbie felt sick. She swayed on her feet. She'd already suspected it, and now she had his confession: Logan had caused the zombie siege that had wiped out her village. He'd done it on purpose.

"How could you?" she breathed. "How could you do something so . . . so . . ."

"Brilliant," said Ben.

"Ben!" Bobbie said, appalled.

He turned to her. "I'm sorry, Bobbie, but you've got to admit . . . it's a clever way of doing things. Set aside morality for a minute," he said. "Put your personal feelings away and look at it objectively."

"I can't do that," she said. "Our morality is part of us, Ben. You can't just switch it off . . ."

Or *could* he? Bobbie's heart sank. She'd been sure that Ben was better than this.

Part of her had known the truth, though. Hadn't she? It was why she still hadn't told him she lost the emeralds.

"I'm expanding, Ben," continued Logan. "The truth is, the operation's gotten a little *big*, and the Ravagers could use a little more help. Iron farms are the wave of the future, and I intend to set up farms for interested clients overseas. I could use someone like you on my team." Logan leveled Ben with a very serious look, leaning forward on his obsidian throne. "I need to know I can trust you, though."

"Of course you can trust me," said Ben.

"Not as long as you're with *her*," said Logan. He ran his hand along the scepter. "And don't blame me. I've been nothing but hospitable. *She's* the one who's being stubborn."

If he thought Bobbie had been stubborn so far, he hadn't seen anything yet. She took a step forward, ready to pull him right off that throne of his.

Then she noticed something. The "scepter" beside the throne . . . it was familiar. It looked just like the switch they'd seen in the tunnel. What had Ben called it?

"Ben, is that—"

Bobbie's question died on her lips. As she had turned toward her friend, she saw something she never thought she'd see.

Ben was aiming an arrow. At *her*.

"Ben?" she said. "What are you doing?"

"I'm sorry, Bobbie," he said. "Really. It's been fun, but . . . I just got an offer I can't refuse."

"Don't do this, Ben," Bobbie pleaded. "I know you think he's your friend. But you aren't blind. You can see how cruel he is, can't you?" She shook her head. "Maybe you think you deserve his cruelty. Maybe you think you can fix him. I don't know." She leveled him with a steely look. "I'm telling you that you deserve better than this. That you *are* better than this. And that together—you and me?" She smiled. "We can stop everything that's happening here. We can make the world *better*, instead of just trying to be the richest, fiercest survivor."

"I'm . . . I'm sorry, Bobbie. I promise you, this isn't personal," Ben assured her, and he pulled the bowstring taut. "Well, I guess it's a *little* personal. You did shoot me with an arrow the first time we met."

"Ben, think about this!"

But Ben didn't stop to think. He let the arrow fly.

It struck Bobbie in the shoulder, knocking her back.

She dropped Johnny's lead. She tried to keep her balance.

But the cliff—

She fell off the edge of the cliff.

And she didn't stop falling until she splashed into the ocean.

CHAPTER 35

When Bobbie opened her eyes, she was deep underwater. This was not what she'd meant when she said she wanted to see the ocean.

Her heart held a chaotic swirl of emotions. She was angry and confused. She was hurt—in more ways than one.

But she was in awe, too, of the sight that greeted her.

An alien landscape spread below her, like a desert covered in a hazy blue fog, with long, swaying strands of sparse grass and little green tubes that glowed with an inner light. A school of colorful fish swam up to her as if curious and then, when she reached out to touch them, they darted away. One fish, riddled with spines and startled by all the movement, puffed up to epic proportions. In the distance, a multi-armed squid drifted lazily. It looked like it was flying.

Bobbie forgot her anger and her worry. The world was so big— but it didn't make her feel small. It made her feel as if there were as many possibilities for her as there were stars in the sky.

But every possible future started with getting Johnny back. She wouldn't let Logan and Ben use her brother as a tool to hurt others.

Bobbie gritted her teeth, pulling Ben's arrow from her shoulder. She decided then and there that she'd make him eat that stupid glowing sword of his. He'd regret the combat lessons he'd given her, that was for certain.

She began swimming for the surface, but then thought better of it. Logan and Ben probably assumed she was dead, and why disabuse them of that? She didn't seem to be having much trouble holding her breath, so she took a moment to consider her options. What if she dug her way to safety?

Bobbie swam to a sheer rock wall and started digging. The water slowed her swings somewhat, but all the same, the diamond pickaxe made short work of the stone as she carved a narrow tunnel forward, and then up. By the time she felt the need to take a breath, she was out of the water and lost, somewhere, deep underground.

But she was alive. And she had a mission.

"I'm coming for you, Johnny," she said. "And if I have to go through that traitor to get you . . . then that's what I'll do."

It was late morning by the time she'd made it to the surface. Rather than rush in to save Johnny—which she desperately wanted to do—she decided to play it smart. Ben had told her that battles were won with intelligence, not swords. Just as she'd watched and learned the attack patterns of creepers, zombies, and slimes, she could benefit from watching Logan's fortress at a distance and striking only when the moment was right.

At dusk, she finally saw what she'd been waiting for. The gate opened, and Logan's cronies appeared, leaving on their nightly errand to check Logan's traps and round up any zombies they could find. As soon as they were out of sight, Bobbie made her move, staying out of view of the main gate and hacking her way into the fortress from the far side of the mountain.

As she stalked the spartan hallways of Logan's fortress, she took a grim pleasure in the irony: This time, *she* was invading *his* home. And she'd help herself to all of his stuff.

She found a chest in an empty bedroom. It was booby-trapped — Ben had taught her what to look for, and she avoided the trap, taking the TNT that had been rigged to blow, as well as the various valuables she found inside the chest. She didn't even have a use for most of it, but depriving Logan was reason enough.

After a few more rooms — and a few more booby-trapped chests — Bobbie found Ben, sleeping soundly in one of the many identical bedrooms. She closed the door behind her — and kicked him out of the bed.

"Slimeballs!" he said, rubbing the sleep from his eyes. And then — to Bobbie's surprise — he smiled. "Thank goodness!" he said. "I spent half the day looking for you." Bobbie glared at him, and he fidgeted nervously. "Uh, so how are you? You look good. All that iron really . . . brings out the steely resolve in your eyes . . ."

"Save it," said Bobbie, and she shoved her sword under his chin. "The only thing I want to hear from you is where I can find Johnny."

Ben raised his arms and looked nervously at the blade. "He's perfectly safe! He's in the pit. With all the other zombies."

"He's safe," Bobbie said, unamused. "Surrounded by zombies."

"They won't hurt him. I watched him to be sure. He only seems to fight other zombies when *you're* endangered by them." Ben swallowed hard. "That's why I shot you—it was the only way I could save you both."

"My hero," Bobbie said.

"Honest! Didn't you see that redstone torch? The one by Logan's throne?" Ben put one hand on her blade, gently pushing it away. "We were on a trapdoor the whole time. You, me, and Johnny. If I hadn't played along—if I hadn't said and done *everything* he wanted—we would have all tumbled down into that pit."

"So instead of falling into the zombie pit *together*, I took a surprise swim all by myself," said Bobbie. "I'm lucky I didn't drown."

"It wasn't luck," Ben said. "Didn't you notice how long you were able to stay underwater without breathing? Didn't you think that was weird?"

Bobbie narrowed her eyes. "What are you getting at?"

"I shot you, yes," he said. "But I shot you with one of my special arrows. It was tipped with a Potion of Water Breathing!" Ben shook his head. "I hated to do it. But I knew you'd be okay. And now, because of that, Logan trusts me. I can sabotage him from the inside!"

Bobbie finally lowered her sword. "So he bought it."

"Yes!" said Ben. "Unfortunately, so did Johnny. Your brother did not take kindly to my little display. So he ended up in the pit, and I ended up having breakfast with Logan." Ben gazed off wistfully. "Cake for breakfast. You would have loved it."

"I'm sure."

"The conversation was dreadful, though. He's done here, Bobbie. He's wiped out every village within fifty thousand blocks." Ben clambered to his feet. "He's taking his army and marching east."

"East?" echoed Bobbie. "But east of here . . ."

"Is the ocean," Ben finished. "He's going off the edge of the map. He's going to find a whole new *continent* to plunder."

The world was so big, Bobbie remembered. Full of mystery and adventure.

And it should stay that way.

"We have to stop him," she said.

"Yeah!" Ben said. "That's what I've been trying to figure out. The obvious solution is to destroy his army of zombies. But how to do that, I don't know."

"Would this help?" Bobbie asked, and she held up one of her recently acquired blocks of TNT.

"Careful with that!" said Ben, and he flinched. But then a smile spread across his face. "All those zombies in one place. Minecarts that lead right to them. And some TNT." He nodded. "I can work with that. But you'll have to get Johnny out of there. We'll need to time it all perfectly."

"Wait a minute," said Bobbie. "So *my* part of the plan is to walk into a pit full of hundreds of zombies in the moments before the whole place blows up and find the one zombie we want to save?"

"He'll be easy to find," said Ben. "He's the shortest zombie there by far."

"That actually makes him *harder* to spot," Bobbie argued. "And I'll stick out like a blue axolotl."

"Not if you're invisible."

Bobbie grinned. "You have Potions of Invisibility?"

"Well," said Ben. "Sort of." And he held up an arrow.

Bobbie's smile fell away. "If we get out of this alive . . . we have *got* to brew some normal potions."

CHAPTER 36

Bobbie had five arrows tipped with Invisibility+. That meant she had exactly five minutes of invisibility. Five minutes to find her favorite zombie in a sea of *hundreds*.

Five minutes before the explosions started, and Logan's army was reduced to ashes and rotten flesh.

Bobbie removed her iron armor—a necessary risk, for the invisibility effect to work—and waited atop Logan's platform. From here, she'd have a perfect view of the moment the sun peeked above the horizon. That would be the signal to begin.

In the meantime, Bobbie turned to consider Logan's massive obsidian throne. It was an ugly thing—it captured his despotic spirit almost too well. And hadn't Ben said that obsidian was useful?

She pulled out the diamond pickaxe he'd lent her, and she smiled. Logan's throne would make a fine souvenir.

She had just stashed the last piece of obsidian in her inventory when the sun appeared. It was time. Bobbie drank a potion—Ben had snuck down to the castle's courtyard and brewed it just for her—and then she activated a redstone torch. The floor dropped out from beneath her—but the Potion of Slow Falling she'd just guzzled ensured a gentle descent into the pit below. As she drifted lower, and the crush of zombies drew near, Bobbie couldn't help thinking of Ben's traumatic story. Just as he'd been stuck in the webs, sinking ever so slowly toward certain death, Bobbie found her anxiety growing as she neared the end of her descent.

A moment before she touched down, she pricked herself with an arrow, disappearing from view.

The monstrous mobs were wandering aimlessly, bouncing off the walls and each other, waiting for the moment when Logan would next set them loose against an unsuspecting world. They didn't know she was there—a part of her had feared they'd smell her, sense her somehow—but she was safe to move among them, and she moved quickly but carefully, not wanting to touch them but needing to cover a lot of ground.

She was looking for Johnny. And it wasn't long before she found a familiar face.

It wasn't Johnny's face, however.

"Cleric Avery?!"

For a moment, Bobbie forgot that she was in mortal danger. The shock of seeing her old neighbor was enough to make her blurt out their name—alerting them, momentarily, to her presence. But, turning toward her and seeing only empty air, Cleric Avery continued on their way.

Which was lucky. Because Cleric Avery was a zombie.

It all made a twisted sort of sense to Bobbie. The tunnels leading from this pit—the ones that ran beneath villages, including her own—they weren't just there to get zombies into the villages.

They were there to get zombies out, too.

That's how Logan had grown his army to such an impressive size. He'd probably started with just a handful of captive zombies. But once those zombies had infected villagers, their numbers grew. And the more villages they attacked, the larger the force became.

She saw Farmer Briar in the crowd, too. Her entire village was here—her neighbors, her friends, her *parents*—all conscripted into Logan's vile service, forced to do the bidding of the boy who'd betrayed them.

Bobbie's invisibility wore off. As quick as lightning, she pricked herself with a new arrow.

One minute was already gone.

In four more minutes . . . Ben's explosions would destroy Logan's army.

Including everyone Bobbie had ever known.

CHAPTER 37

Bobbie had to act fast if she was going to thwart Ben's plan. There was no way she could reach him in time—but the explosions? She could stop the explosions.

Probably.

Maybe.

There were three tunnels leading into the pit. Three directions from which Ben would be sending minecarts full of TNT.

His plan had been to start in the south tunnel and work his way around to the north. So that's where Bobbie had to start, too.

She ran as fast as she could, getting dangerously close to zombies as she went. They startled and growled when she got too close, suspicious that an intruder was among them—but she remained invisible and on the move, so their grasping arms found only empty air.

It was reckless, but what choice did she have?

She used a third arrow. She had three minutes left to save them all.

At the southernmost tunnel, she paused only a moment before deciding on a course of action. Stone wouldn't do enough to block the blast created by the oncoming minecart. But *obsidian* could be strong enough to do the job.

She blocked off the tunnel, then ran toward the next one.

Arrow four of five extended her invisibility for another minute.

She saw a zombified Shepherd Ellis in the crowd, and it spurred her on, pushing her to move faster than ever.

But the pit was so large. And even though she was running at a reckless clip, the sheer mass of zombies slowed her down. By the time she'd plugged the second tunnel with obsidian, her invisibility was already wearing off.

She did the math. She couldn't make it to the final tunnel in time.

Was two out of three good enough? A single explosion wouldn't destroy many of the zombies. But it would destroy some— whichever poor souls happened to be in the vicinity of the northern tunnel.

What if her brother was over there? Or her parents?

The answer came to her just as she pulled the fifth and final arrow of invisibility from her inventory. If she couldn't stop the explosion, she needed to get the zombies away from it.

For that, she needed bait.

She let the fifth arrow drop to the ground, unused.

She quickly donned her iron armor, tapping her helmet for good luck.

And then she took a deep breath.

"Hey, zombies!" she shouted. "Come and get me!"

It worked. Every zombie in the pit was instantly moving in her direction.

It was like the siege on her village all over again—but exponentially worse. The sheer number of zombies was panic inducing. She kept her back to the wall and focused on her combat training, staying on the defensive, knocking the mobs back whenever they stepped into range. But she was at a disadvantage, and not only because she was outnumbered. She feared hitting any single zombie more than once, worried about doing any permanent damage to anyone who might be curable.

And then she was struck by an arrow.

"Ow!" she cried, and she scanned the pit for the source of the attack. Was there a skeleton hiding among the zombies?

She saw the second arrow in time to duck it. The projectile came not from the horde, but from above.

She looked up to see Logan seething at her from his balcony.

"How are you still alive?" he said through clenched teeth. "What do you think you're *doing* down there?"

He didn't wait for an answer, firing off a third arrow instead. Bobbie dodged it—but stepped right into the swiping claws of the nearest zombie.

Her survival had already been unlikely. Now it seemed impossible. Her rhythm was off, and she couldn't hope to avoid ranged and melee attacks at the same time. She took another hit, and then another. The iron armor helped, but not nearly enough. It could only soak up so much damage.

A cold dread settled into Bobbie's heart. She knew she couldn't hold out much longer.

Then came the explosion. The north side of the pit erupted in fire and smoke. The zombies turned toward the commotion, distracted, and so did Logan. Bobbie tried to slip away—

Too slow. The nearest zombies pressed in on her. They

grasped, they bit, and they tore. She pushed herself against the wall, so they couldn't come at her from every direction. But she was overwhelmed by sheer numbers . . . and, worse, with the knowledge that she had failed. In saving the zombies, she had only guaranteed they would remain in Logan's clutches.

So, really, she hadn't saved anyone.

Through the horde, she could see Logan leering at her from above. He made no effort to help her. There was no reason to think that he *would*, but somehow, Bobbie found his callous inaction more horrifying than the zombies themselves. The undead mobs were only remaining true to their nature. But what could twist a *person* to make him so monstrous?

Suddenly, Logan lurched backward. An arrow had lodged itself in his shoulder, and a look of fury settled onto his face.

"Traitor!" he cried. "What do you think you're doing?!"

The zombies closest to Bobbie were knocked aside, and all of a sudden, Ben was standing before her. "I'm doing the right thing," Ben said, and though the words were directed at Logan, his eyes were on Bobbie. "What happened?" he asked her, and he quickly placed fences down to give them some breathing room. "This wasn't the plan."

"Careful with that sword!" she warned him. "Some of these zombies are my friends."

Ben let out a brief laugh. "I *knew* you were a zombie lover."

Another explosion rang out, and the entire fortress seemed to tremble.

"What was *that*?" cried Logan.

"That was your bedroom," Ben called up to him. "If you hurry, you might be able to salvage some of your loot. The stuff I didn't steal, I mean . . ."

Logan grimaced. "This isn't over," he said. "You'll both be

sorry." He glared at them from above. "You know I always get even." Then he turned and ran off.

Bobbie frowned. "I think you bought us some time," she said. "But you didn't exactly break the cycle of plundering."

"I know messing with his stuff wasn't part of the plan." Ben shrugged. "I had some extra TNT and a grudge. It doesn't make me a bad guy, does it?"

Before Bobbie could answer, a pint-size zombie leaped from the throng, landing on Ben's back and tearing at his hair.

"Johnny!" said Bobbie.

"Ow!" cried Ben. "Get this flesh-crazed toddler off of me!"

"Johnny, it's okay," said Bobbie, and she pulled her brother off. He continued kicking and punching at the air, in Ben's general direction. "He's our friend! He didn't really hurt me. Much."

"Ditto," Ben said, rubbing his head. "Now can we please get out of here?" The zombies pressed against the fence, gnashing their teeth and slamming their fists against the frail wood. "Otherwise, I'm going to end up giving your zombie friends a terrible case of indigestion, and I know you wouldn't like that."

They cut their way through stone, looping around to one of the tunnels that had been blocked off with obsidian. The TNT had done massive damage, but Ben was able to repair the redstone mechanism while Bobbie crafted a couple of minecarts, which she placed on the rails beyond the blast zone.

"Ben, I have a confession to make," said Bobbie, and she lowered her brother into one of the carts. "The fee I promised you . . . I can't pay. I left the emeralds in a chest, back when we were mining for gold."

"Yeah . . . I know," said Ben.

Bobbie was shocked. "You knew? How?"

Ben shrugged. "I was keeping an eye on you. I saw you stash them there."

"And you stayed anyway." Bobbie smiled. "You could have left us. But you didn't. Even knowing I couldn't pay you." She threw her arms around him. "Oh, I knew you were a good person."

"Yeah, well," said Ben. "I guess I have a confession to make, too." He held up an emerald. "Once I saw where you stashed the emeralds, I sort of helped myself to them."

Bobbie's jaw dropped. "You—you jerk!"

"Hey!" said Ben. "Hold on. Your original point still stands. I could have left you two at any point. I'd already gotten paid!"

"I guess that's true," said Bobbie grudgingly.

Ben held out his arms for another hug. "So all's forgiven?"

"Sure," said Bobbie, and she shoved him—hard enough to knock him into the empty minecart next to Johnny's.

Ben laughed—and then he saw Bobbie had put her hand to the redstone torch. "Bobbie," he said carefully. "What are you doing?"

"You're the only one I can trust to keep him safe," she answered.

"We'll keep him safe together," Ben insisted.

Bobbie shook her head. Tears glistened in her eyes. "Logan's not going to stop, Ben. He's going to take everyone I care about away, across an ocean, and use them to hurt other people. I have to find a way to stop him. To save everyone!" She wiped away a single tear. "But I can't keep putting Johnny in danger. He needs to stay far, far away from Logan."

"You both do," Ben argued. "You don't know him like I do. He's dangerous!"

"That's why I have to do this, Ben," she said.

And then she activated the switch.

"Bobbie, stop!" cried Ben as the minecarts pulled away.

Johnny growled mournfully.

"Take care of each other!" she called back. "Don't stop looking for a cure. I'll see you both again one day!"

She let herself watch, just for a moment, as Ben and Johnny sped away from her into the darkness.

And then she turned her attention back to the task at hand.

Her village had been destroyed. But there was still a chance to save the people who had lived there.

And in the end, wasn't that what made a home? Not the place, but the people?

Home wasn't lost to her. It wasn't in her past.

It was ahead of her. And she would do anything to save it.

ACKNOWLEDGMENTS

As any horror fan knows, the very best zombie stories aren't just about flesh-eating hordes of the undead. They're about *community*—about how people come together (or fail to) in the face of an existential threat.

In that spirit, I want to acknowledge that this book wouldn't exist if not for the tireless efforts of many talented people working together.

My thanks, first and foremost, go to editor Alex Davis, who came to me with an irresistible, undeniably cool pitch. Everything I love about this book is traceable directly to his vision, and in my moments of doubt, anxiety, or flubbed deadlines, his encouragement, insights, and patience kept me moving in the right direction. I'm thrilled that this is just the start of our collaboration.

Thanks to all the awesome people at Mojang, who have entrusted me to tell stories in their wild and wonderful (Over) world—and especially to Alex Wiltshire, who always comes through with a great suggestion just when I need it the most. (And who has forgiven me for somehow consistently forgetting to capitalize Enderman. See? I'm learning!)

Thanks to Kaz Oomori and Elizabeth A. D. Eno for the chilling cover and package, which so perfectly capture the spirit of the book—while evoking some of my major zombie-related influences. (Shout-out to the late, great George Romero.)

Thanks to the copy editors, proofreaders, managing editors, and various support staff working behind the scenes at Penguin Random House. They are the unsung heroes behind all our favorite books—and, in the case of this book, they hit some pretty gnarly deadlines in order to give me as much time as possible. I appreciate that more than I can say.

Thanks to Dennis Shealy, my editor on the Woodsword Chronicles and Stonesword Saga books, for inviting me to tell stories in this wonderful sandbox to begin with, and for putting me on Alex's radar.

Thanks to my agents, Josh and Tracey Adams, who have helped make so many of my dreams come true.

Thanks to Andrew Eliopulos, my co-adventurer in all things, who keeps me clothed, fed, and happy when I've overextended myself, and who helped me iron out a few particularly tricky worldbuilding details. Andrew, I would be a shambling monstrosity without you!

Thanks to the young readers, parents, grandparents, teachers, and librarians who have reached out to me to express their enjoyment of Woodsword Chronicles or Stonesword Saga. Your kind words (and illustrations!) make it all worthwhile. I hope that some of you have followed me over to this series.

Finally, a special thanks to my dear friend, John Jennison—horror fan, creative powerhouse, and steadfast cheerleader. This one is for you, buddy.

ABOUT THE AUTHOR

NICK ELIOPULOS is a professional writer, editor, game designer, and teacher. (He likes to keep busy.) He is the author of two officially licensed Minecraft chapter book series, the Woodsword Chronicles and the Stonesword Saga, as well as the co-author of the Adventurers Guild trilogy. Nick was born in Florida, lives in New York, and spends most of his free time in the Nether.

nickeliopulos.com
Twitter: @NickEliopulos

ABOUT THE TYPE

This book was set in Electra, a typeface designed for Linotype by W. A. Dwiggins, the renowned type designer (1880–1956). Electra is a fluid typeface, avoiding the contrasts of thick and thin strokes that are prevalent in most modern typefaces.

DISCOVER MORE MINECRAFT:
Have You Read Them All?

- ☐ *The Island* by Max Brooks
- ☐ *The Crash* by Tracey Baptiste
- ☐ *The Lost Journals* by Mur Lafferty
- ☐ *The End* by Catherynne M. Valente
- ☐ *The Voyage* by Jason Fry
- ☐ *The Rise of the Arch-Illager* by Matt Forbeck
- ☐ *The Shipwreck* by C. B. Lee
- ☐ *The Mountain* by Max Brooks
- ☐ *The Dragon* by Nicky Drayden
- ☐ *Mob Squad* by Delilah S. Dawson
- ☐ *The Haven Trials* by Suyi Davies
- ☐ *Mob Squad: Never Say Nether* by Delilah S. Dawson

Penguin
Random
House